PRAISE FOR THE FORGETTING NAVIGATIONS

"Few writers can face brutality without flinching, and fewer can tell it well. Marlee Jane Ward is that rare author who can show you the worst that humanity can do, and at the same time, give you something beautiful. This book is a tapestry of blood, grief, and unbreakable love."

—Meg Elison, author of *The Book of the Unnamed Midwife*

"Harrowing. Thrilling. Beautifully life-affirming. The Forgetting Navigations is all of these things and more. Marlee Jane Ward uses the grammar of space opera to tell an unforgettable story of what it takes to survive in a harsh universe as a woman, and in the process confirms herself as a major new author to watch."

—Charlie Jane Anders, author of *Lessons in Magic and Disaster*

"The Forgetting Navigations offers a clear-eyed understanding of the screaming horrors that frame the borders of our world—but also of the oasis that can be found on the eye of the storm. In these pages, Ward skillfully navigates the difficult terrain of real pain and grief to remind us that peace and recovery are still possible, that kind people do exist, and that all of these demand to be protected and fought for and treasured when we find them."

—Aimee Ogden, author of *Local Star*

THE FORGETTING NAVIGATIONS

MARLEE JANE WARD

This is a work of fiction. All of the characters, organizations, and events portrayed are either products of the author's imagination or used fictitiously.

THE FORGETTING NAVIGATIONS

Edited by Holly Lyn Walrath.

Cover design by Holly Lyn Walrath

Published by Interstellar Flight Press

Houston, Texas.

www.interstellarflightpress.com

ISBN (Print): 978-1-953736-55-0

ISBN (EBook): 978-1-953736-54-3

First Edition: 2026

For anyone who feels adrift—I hope you find your tether.

CONTENT WARNINGS

Violence
Allusions to sexual assault
Mentions of mutilation
Mentions of self harm

CONTENTS

THE FORGETTING NAVIGATIONS

[1]

My chances in the lifepod are fifty-fifty, but I'll take those odds.

The second he unlocks me, I take my chance. I tear out of his grasp, my sweaty skin slipping through his fingers, and I run. The fear makes me fast but loose, and I bounce off the cold steel hallway walls. The bridge is so close, and I tumble into it, hitting the button for the door and then jamming the auto-open function by mashing the number pad with my palm. It always takes a moment for the system to correct. I have no idea if I will be able to access the ship's nav system, but the screen is unlocked, so I press it with adrenaline-trembling fingers. I need to get us out of warp, or the lifepod will be torn apart by the warp bubble. I can hear him pummeling the bridge door, trying to open it. I keep making errors on the screen, my mind frayed and my hands shaking. I finally navigate to the right place, but just as I'm confirming the action, the door opens. I race across the bridge to the escape pod.

Slamming into the lifepod at full speed, I lose my senses for a moment, lose my lead. I turn to see him reaching for me, the glint of the knife gripped in his other hand. In my mind, I hear the *shick* sound his blade makes as it unsheathes. It sings through my head; I'll never not hear it. I hit the button for the door, but he jams it with his arm. The steel grips his wrist, still trying to close, and he bellows like a wild animal. I see his eyes flash through the gap in the door. They were empty before, so void and cold as he gripped my jaw and held the tip of the knife to my eyelid, a hushed voice in my ear, *don't move, don't make a sound.* Now, they're full of hatred. Fire hot.

Then he pulls his arm out, and the door slams home. I slip into the launch sling and slap the big red evac button with my palm. The acceleration sucks me back, making the straps feel loose, too loose. I clench my teeth and ride the rattle and bang, then things go quiet and smooth as the lifepod pops out of the belly of the ship.

I hold my breath, watching the blips on the info panel as the distance between us widens. Then his ship disappears, dropping off the sensors and into warp again.

I'm safe now.

I'm safe now, aren't I?

I wait, weightless. The pod doesn't have a grav panel, so I watch my hair float around my face for a while. Blood lifts from the graze on my knee and floats, spherical. The spicy, metallic smell mingles with the musty stink of canned air. The only sound is my breath that shortens until I surrender to the gravity of it all, the relief and fear, and I sob, sob, sob. I don't like to cry, and usually there's no time or room in my life for emotion or other inessential things, but the ampy surge of adrenaline and the hollow of its absence wrecks me, scoops me out, and I can't help it. There's no one to see, hear, or punish me for these tears, so I let go, let my body override my brain for just one moment, to feel and cry. The tears surge into spheres, too, joining the blood to float around in the small space of the pod. But crying doesn't change anything, so I stop after a while.

This is a standard shipping route, so some passenger liner or cargo run will come along soon and lock a beam on me. It can't take that long.

Can it?

Time passes and my thoughts get big enough to fill the space. One phrase starts to circle lazily in my mind, sometimes widening into an orbit around me and sometimes spinning fast enough to make its own gravity: *how the fuck are you going to get out of this one, Evey Et?*

The walls are dull steel, seamed, and riveted. There's a pair of launch slings behind me, upholstered in dusty yellow with harnesses twisting gently in the zero grav. The hatch is in front, smooth and cool to the touch. Beyond that, infinite vacuum. There's enough room inside the pod for two if no one moves around, and it's my lifeline, but it feels like something else.

it's a coffin, it's my coffin, it's a pressure-hulled vessel for my dead body

Between the launch slings is an info panel. The pod has life support for two people for a week, the levels showing in green bars, full and glowing across the screen. With just me, there's extra air, water, and food, but only enough fuel to keep the pod warm for seven days, and I can't eat or drink or breathe the extra rations if I'm frozen solid. There isn't anything else in the pod except a medkit in a slot beneath the info panel. It has nothing in it besides one of those crinkly silver blankets, so I wrap it around myself, covering my nakedness from no one.

and I try not to think about why I am naked, or how, or what for

This pod is my world now. I stop knowing if it's worse or better than being alone on the ship with him.

I'd do anything for a window. No, not anything, but a lot. Who knows, maybe the view across the galaxy would be worse than the view of close steel. Maybe the stillness of space would curdle my mind. But with a clear diamond port or even a glitchy viewscreen, I could see something approaching. I could count stars. I could lose myself in the dark. I could counter the claustrophobic press of the steel walls with something, anything. Instead, it's just me and my memories, floating in the harsh-lit pod. The good ones I can lose myself in. My collection is small, and precious. The bad memories I try to keep in boxes, wrapped up tight. They pile up, spill over. I wish I could blast them out of an airlock, let the universe have them.

I got a little tug in my gut when he said yes. I needed the ride; I always needed a ride, but I always listened to my gut, too. This time, I took the ride when I knew I shouldn't and I'd paid, I'd paid.

I had to get the fuck off K21. It rained all day and night, and I'd had two run-ins with the Force already. No one was offering rides, so there were a few of us lurking at the docks, watching for kindly looking crew, or anyone already scanning the port for us, needing us as much as we needed them.

The more of us there were trying to scrounge up rides, the more likely the Force would be on us, like they didn't have anything better to do. They were pissed to be assigned to immigration and customs duty and took it out on whoever they could. I was good at blending in; we all did our best, but sometimes they just knew. Maybe they could tell we didn't belong by the look in our eyes.

His ship was a C-class hauler, a steel crescent in the launch sling, bots crawling over it to join the giant cargo hold. It looked like a cow tick I picked off myself once, the hauler like the tiny head and the cargo holds like the body, swollen massive with blood. I couldn't help but think of that engorged tick whenever I saw a hauler at the dock.

The man was friendly enough. He introduced himself as Carter, he, and shook my hand. He was an unremarkable-looking person, brown eyes and dark curly hair. He was tall and lean, and I could tell he was wiry with muscle under his navy coverall.

I asked him what he wanted for the ride to Seris, and he gave me a look.

"What do you mean?" he asked.

I blinked a few times. "In return for the ride. I like to negotiate that right away."

"What makes you think I want something in return?"

"Everyone wants something in return," I said. "Why would they do it for nothing?"

"Maybe out of pity?" he said softly. It was a question, but he wasn't asking me. Then he blinked a few times and said, "You can help me with the cargo."

"Deal," I said. We shook. Something pulled gently in my stomach. I ignored it and followed him aboard.

It's hard to keep the memories boxed up in this unbearable isolation, the infinite fucking quiet. I spend a while in the pod wishing that the endlessly gleaming light would go out and then breathless hours hoping that it doesn't, doesn't plunge me into a black so deep I know I'd start to bleed into it, or it would bleed into me. Then I wish for a middle ground, something soft and gentle to ease the glaring bounce of cold white light off dull steel. Just so I can fucking sleep. I hang mid-pod in the bright light, in such deep silence that I think I can hear the glug of blood moving through my veins, loud enough to keep me awake. But when I do sleep, I wake screaming to visions of the hatch opening to him and his void eyes, and I take a while to promise myself that he's not waiting just on the other side of that steel door. That there's nothing outside but the gentle vacuum of space.

but how would I know? how can I know anything from in here?

Nothing continues to happen. Space is like that. Time is different everywhere, but it is longest in space. In the spaces between suns, planets, time gets stretchy. One girl in one lifepod for one week is nothing, *nothing*, is of no consequence to the vastness of the universe. Time is short for humans, though, and it is shortest for me in here. I can only tell the passing of time from the levels, which I watch and watch. They are all I have to look at; they are the best show in town. Often, I am still, floating gently in the middle of the pod, eyes locked to the levels. Sometimes, I spin in the air, making a game for myself to not hit the walls, see how many revolutions I can go without smacking my knee into the hatch. Occasionally I break after playing this game too long, screaming and thrashing my body into the steel until I'm bruised, and then I watch the colors on my limbs and torso change from blue to black and purple, brown and yellow, and it gives me something to look at. The bruises amuse me, and the pain makes me feel like I'm still alive in here. I have nothing else to hurt myself with, though I try to use the crinkly silver blanket like paper, try to slice myself with the edge of it. It's too soft. I resort to raking my fingernails up my legs and arms, my torso. The sting and the blood under my nails feels real. But I can't do anything to hasten my death, not unless I want to batter myself against the steel. Better to wait for my body temperature to drop and drop. It will be cold, but I don't think it will hurt.

I can't wait.

I have to.

He waited until we slipped into warp.

In the moment after I saw the warp bubble form, stars bending around the edges of the view, I felt a weight lift to know that I was moving. Sometimes I wished that I could stay in warp forever, fast and quiet in the little bubble of condensed space. I felt hidden there, like I was safer somehow. Like I didn't exist. I always wondered what that meant.

We were on the bridge, him at the controls and me staring out at the view, stars curving. He'd been mostly friendly, so I tried a little conversation.

"I like being in warp. Feels so quiet," I shared. He didn't reply, only stood up, turning around to look at me, and what I saw made my heart start to slam against my ribs. His eyes were so cold and void. They were black, not the steady brown I'd seen in the pale glow of K21's twin stars. They were like black holes sucking in all the light. The edges of his lips danced slightly. Fear trickled through my limbs, hot and liquid. I wanted to vomit. I wanted to scream or to run, but there was no one to hear me and nowhere to go.

"No," I said, my voice small and crackly. I said it so that later, when I didn't have the voice to say it, it would have been said. He just laughed.

I thought of other times I'd felt fear like that, seen eyes grow angry, seen them shine with the dual glimmer of desire and fury. Those memories were nothing. His eyes told me about a pain and indignity like nothing I'd known before, and I was an old hand at those.

My body continues to function, and I continue to care for it, mostly out of habit. On day six, or thereabouts, I defecate into one of the flimsy bags provided in the waste unit, then put it into the receptacle. It jams, catching the edge of the bag in the hinge and ripping it open in the process. I gag, try to catch it, miss, and then begin to scream as the shit does what shit does in zero gravity. The receptacle hatch won't close, and I try to keep all the other waste bags in, stuffing my crinkly silver blanket in there, but several get through and tear open as I frantically try to catch them. In moments, the whole pod is contaminated, including the food and water. I gag, then vomit, catching it in a bag from the waste unit, even though I don't know why. This final indignity breaks me. I curl into the smallest ball I can, globes of piss and shit orbiting me, and I wish I was fucking dead.

My hair is wretched, snakes of foulness weaving around my face. I can't smell anything anymore. I can't hear anything or see anything. I don't bother moving or speaking. I am nothing. I am floating organic matter, like the rest of what's in here.

I've felt alone for most of my life, but never so acutely as I do now. The distance between me and *anyone* else is almost infinite. I can feel it, the vastness, like my fingers reaching out and out forever, touching nothing.

When the blips start to sound, I think I'm delirious. I'm filthy, floating, and wide-eyed, hovering somewhere between asleep and awake, dead and alive. I am both and neither. I am Schrodinger's girl, simultaneous until you open my pod.

you're hearing things, Evey.

I've been hearing things for a while. Voices, chanting like songs, prayers. Slow, deep rhythms, coming from all sides. My mother. My little sister wailing, *don't leave me, Evey.* Quiet instructions, my screams ragged in the hush of space. *Don't move, don't make a sound.* The endless *shick* of blades unsheathing. There's nowhere to escape the noise.

Now my brain is making up blips, so I refuse to listen, turn mid-pod away from the sound, and try to shake it out of my head, my ears.

NO, EVEY, DO YOU HEAR THAT?

it's not real.

IT IS EVEY, DO YOU HEAR IT?

Something has dropped out of warp right next to the lifepod. It picked up my distress signal and didn't ignore it, it hasn't just blinked past. Hot, fast hope races through my bloodstream like a kid bouncing off the walls of a ship corridor. I make my eyes focus. Up until now, there hadn't been a point, so I'd let them go lazy. I wipe piss and shit off the info panel.

There, a shape. A ship. A big one. Passenger ship? Cargo hauler? Is it the Force? Is it *him*? Has he come back for me? I bump into the wall as the ship locks onto the lifepod and starts to reel me in. The fuel level is in the red. I hadn't bothered looking at it for a while. I didn't want to know.

There's a noise, a real noise, as my pod locks to their dock. The fear screams in my head alongside the sound. My mind flickers with possibilities, images and scenarios shuffling like cards:

The lock opening to the friendly eyes of an old couple, wrinkled and wizened, ready to nurse me back to myself.

The lock opening to a line of Force officers, guns drawn and screaming GET DOWN, GET DOWN.

The lock opening to the worried staff of a passenger liner, a bus in the black, with a neat, warm infirmary in which to care for me.

The lock opening to *him*, void-eyed and knife drawn.

I can't know. It could be anything, but anything's better than this.

I float up straight, summoning as much dignity as I can, even while globes of my own waste orbit me. The hatch opens without ceremony onto a new world.

I need to see.

———

They rang the bells in the temple when I escaped. I heard the peal of them just before the airlock hissed closed, and I prayed that they wouldn't delay the launch.

I didn't pray to Et, the god who ruled my life in the temple. I had been praying to Et as long as I could remember, but all that brought me was silence. Instead, I prayed to myself. Et wouldn't get me out of this, I would. I'd only recently realized that Et was not real. Et was just power. I had never felt power from any divine source, only from the priests, who used it to get their way. It was too hard for me to believe that what Et wanted was for the priests to treat the acolytes the way they did. Why would something divine want to make us suffer?

I left the night I started menstruating. It was supposed to be a secret ritual, but everyone knew what happened to an acolyte when they began to bleed: the cut. In my head, I heard the *shick* of a blade unsheathing.

On board the first ship leaving Et, the captain told me what he wanted in return for the ride, and I decided that it was preferable to the cut. It was simple, and he was otherwise kind. He taught me card games and Mahjong, and we'd play late into the sleep cycle.

I'd never left the surface of the planet before. I didn't even know what the planet was *called.* All I knew was the prayers, the priests, and my family. I knew the temple stairs under my feet, gilded tiles shimmering in candlelight, and I knew the book of Et from front to back because it was the only book we had.

I can remember bells ringing in the moments before launch, even though that's impossible, even though the sound of the bells couldn't have penetrated the steel hull. They were ringing for me. They rang in my head as the roar of launch ate up everything else.

My heart surges. In the doorway is a tall white person in a plain gray coverall. They've got gray hair shorn close to the scalp, soft wrinkles around their eyes, and are maybe fifteen or so years older than my twenty-five years. They have a blaster holstered, arm cocked, and hand poised to take it out, but when they see me, their hands go up to their mouth. Then their nose.

I reach out and use the edges of the seal to pull myself forward, my filthy hair floating behind me, collecting orbs of waste, and I step into gravity. The force of it takes out my knees, and I crumple to the floor, dragged down by the grav panels. I reconnect with the pull of the ground for a moment, palms flat on the floor. My guts churn, and it hurts my arms to hold myself up, but I'm so grateful for the weight of my body.

Sweet gravity. Sweet air.

"How long have you been in there?" they ask, closing the hatch.

"Seven days," I say, but my voice grabs at my throat. I haven't used it in so long.

They look horrified, but then their face goes back to hawkish and taut so quickly that I wonder if it even happened. "Is there anything you need in there?"

"No. Get rid of it. Please."

They heave the lever and blast away the lifepod, sending it into space so it can hold its secrets alone in the dark forever.

"Let's get you cleaned up," they say, reaching out a hand.

I ignore it. There's no use wasting water cleaning the both of us up. My knees crack and tremble as I follow them to the bathroom. They say nothing about my nakedness or my injuries, and I'm grateful. Their eyes slide right off my body as they open the door to let me in. The shower stall is so small, so bare, like the pod, and I try to box up all the thoughts cascading through my head and thumping through my heart.

But then the water spills out, and it is warm and gentle. The filth sheds with the flow from the shower head, and I spend a quick few minutes and precious water trying to scrub away the memory of his black void eyes, the week in the pod, the week before, my whole life.

I think I am expecting too much of the shower.

When I get out, I can see that they have hung a coverall on a hook for me. Deep green, almost charcoal, it is soft and worn. It smells so clean. It's too big; they are very tall, but I roll the sleeves and cuffs so it doesn't drag, and I pad out of the bathroom unit. My feet leave steam marks on the cold steel floor.

They wait on the bridge, sitting at the control panel, a pair of cups steaming in front of them.

"Do you drink tea?"

I nod, perching on the edge of the panel, and I take the cup, sipping it slowly. It's strong and sweet, and they take it with soy milk.

"Thank you for coming out of warp for me," I say, my voice cracking out of lack of use and emotion.

"No problem," they say, like it was nothing, as if it didn't set their schedule back. Then again, they probably wouldn't have stopped if they were on such a tight turnaround.

"I'm Evey Et. She." The tea soothes my throat and makes my voice less harsh.

"Shirr Krus. She," she offers back.

"This a cargo run?" I ask.

Shirr nods. "Hauling minerals."

I nod and keep sipping my tea. She doesn't ask about the lifepod, or how I got there, and I don't offer. We sit there in silence for a while, watching the stars curve around the warp bubble. It's not an uncomfortable silence. It's just quiet, and it doesn't mean anything.

"Do you have a place to go?" Shirr finally asks.

My brain starts to churn out a story, running back through all my usual lies for the best one, but then I stop. I don't have to. I'm already on the ship.

"Not really. I'll just go wherever you're going."

"It's like that, is it?"

"Yeah."

"Well, I can take you to Seris. It's my next port."

"That's perfect," I say, wondering about Seris and if I'll be able to fit myself out again, seeing as all my stuff is gone. I don't mourn any of my things except the book I wasn't finished reading. I don't need things. I'm my own things.

But thinking of that unfinished book in my backpack makes my thoughts spiral back to my bag, to that ship, to the *shick* of his blade, the cold press of steel against my neck . . . I don't want to think about that. I lock it in, try to coat the memory in layers of forgetting, box it up, and send it out into space.

From the chair, she watches me, sipping from her steaming cup. I think she senses the forgetting navigations I'm doing, but still, she says nothing.

When our tea is finished, Shirr shows me through her ship, *The Algea*.

"The Algea were Greek goddesses. The bringers of tears and pain," she says as she takes me down the hallway. It is steel-walled, seamed, and riveted, but here and there are pictures framed and stuck to the walls at eye height. Paintings, photographs. Art.

"Tears and pain?" I ask.

"I didn't name her," Shirr says. Her smile is close-lipped but not unfriendly. "She came with the name, and it's bad luck to change a ship's name." She stops in front of a door. "This is where you can sleep," she says, opening the door to a small room with a narrow mattress in the corner. The bed is piled high with boxes, old batteries, and spare engine parts. "I'll get that all cleared away for you."

"Thank you," I say. "I'm happy to work for the room."

"I won't say no, I could use the help." She closes the door, my door, and takes me through to the kitchen. It's a homey space, with a table and chairs in the middle. The table is dense black wood, a kind I haven't seen before, the grain deep and the surface smooth with age. The walls are lined with magnetic shelves for bright, mismatched plates and bowls. Garlic hangs in plaits from shelf handles, and there are dusky green, purple, and black herbs drying on a rack over the sink. On one wall, there's a small hydroponic garden, leafy greens and nightshades basking in yellow UV light. There's a book on the table, open to just over halfway through, and a bowl of rice and vegetables. She was reading when she heard my signal. I imagine her hearing the alarm, startling, sitting up taut, placing the book on the table. Less than an hour ago, she was living her quiet life alone, and now I'm here. How does she feel about this? How am I intruding on her life?

In sleep, my hard-won boxes of forgetting all open. I can't control it. They rocket their way back through space. They open, flooding my mind with bad air.

Clammy hands on cool skin.

Don't move, don't make a sound.

Bells. Chanted prayers

The *shick* of blades. Of his knife. Eyes like black holes. Wishing for death to make the pain end, the indignity.

The lifepod. The steel walls. Being alive and dead at the same time.

I wake up screaming.

Footsteps thump across steel, and I'm still not sure where I am, so fear blooms in my gut. When I feel hands on me, trying to gather me up, I fight. They hold tighter, pulling me into a warm body that rocks me gently, and I still struggle now, but less. Shirr murmurs into my hair.

"It's okay. You're safe now."

I want to cling to her, to hold her like she's holding me, but I don't know how, so I just lie against her chest, my own arms wrapped around myself.

Quiet feels different in space. There's our little can of air and sound, outside one big silence. In it, I can hear her heartbeat. It's steady and strong. She is alive.

I am alive.

———

We take the same spots as before. Shirr is in the captain's chair, of course, and I'm perched on the clearest section of the control panel. We both look out at the bending stars, not at each other, and drink tea in perfect silence. She doesn't mention last night, my dreams, the screaming, and I don't either. We sit comfortably in the fable that it didn't happen. Just thinking of it has power, though, and a little flash of memory escapes.

the anguish and the regret the first time he bolted the door to my room was stronger than the physical pain he'd just put me through. a sense of loss echoed around every part of me. the dark and horrific inevitability of my future sucked at every sweet or hopeful thing I had to keep myself warm. I knew I was going to die, and I knew it wasn't going to be easy. I felt so fucking stupid. I felt like I deserved it at the same time as knowing that I didn't. no one could deserve this, no matter what they'd done.

I try to think of Shirr and her arms around my body in the dark. The black tumble slows, stops, and I try to catch the little bubble of memory and fear. Box it. Send it out across the galaxy.

"We're two days out," she tells me. "You know what you'll do once we get to Seris?"

I go to think up a lie, an instinct so deep that it's always my first one, but then I remember that I don't have to bother. There's no grim miner father on Io to make up, no sick grandmother waiting on some prairie planet, or worried mother fretting at my absence. The truth feels so strange when it passes over my lips. I don't know what to do with my face as I say it, don't have the expressions practiced perfectly, so I look out at the stars instead. "Get some supplies. Find some new books. Get another ride."

"Books?"

"Yeah, I like books."

"Are you going somewhere in particular?"

"No. Just gotta keep moving. You know how it is."

She almost nods but doesn't. "You're unregistered." It isn't a question.

"Yeah." I say, my eyes on the floor. "I was born in . . ." My fingers thread through each other, the knuckles going white. Every time I've told anyone that I was born into the cult of Et, they've asked all kinds of questions. Looked at me like I was suddenly something horrific or rarified, and I was never sure which was worse. But Shirr feels like someone who might not look at me that way. "I was born in a cult. They didn't believe in registration."

"Evey *Et*," she says. "You're from the cult of Et?"

"Yeah," I lift my head for a second, meet her eyes. I think she knows I don't want to talk about it, so she doesn't ask any further questions, and I'm grateful. "Anyway, I don't have a chip. I'm not a real person."

"You're a real person," she says. "Why don't you register? Or ... I hear you can purchase valid identities on the black market. Have you thought about that? Finding somewhere safe?"

"I just . . . I'm not sure how to stop. Moving, I mean."

"So, you steal supplies and read books and hitch rides. That's it?"

I move my head in a way that is not quite yes and not quite no.

"Does that life make you happy?"

The question is so unexpected that I look at her before I can stop myself. But then I'm not sure what to say. It takes me a while to figure out how to answer, and I keep looking at her the whole time.

"I think . . ." I start, but that's just to get words started. Otherwise, I might struggle to answer her question forever. The rest comes without thinking, though. "I think being happy is a luxury most people don't get to have."

She purses her lips like she's going to say something, but she doesn't, and we both look out at the view of the black for a while. Finally, I feel her gather her breath to talk.

"What were you reading?"

It is not the question I expected. "What do you mean?"

"Before."

"Oh. Um, Emre Rigan. *The Edge of the Worlds.*"

Shirr laughs, her eyes crinkling at the edges, and I'm so surprised to hear the jagged burst of her laughter that I forget myself and laugh too. "So dry!" she says. "And a brick, too. I made it four chapters and gave up."

"There's always traders in port with a couple of books in with their stuff. Or booksellers, sometimes. But I don't always get to choose what's easiest to take." I shrug and look down at the dregs of the tea. At home, I never drank the last mouthful. Too sweet, always pure sugar. "It was okay, though. I like that Rigan keeps a distance between himself and the information. Gives it a . . ." I can't find the right word.

"Gravity?"

I nod. That's exactly it.

"How far did you get?" she asks.

"About three-quarters through. I'd like to finish it one day."

We sit in silence again. Shir pulls up some charts, looks them over for a while. I stare out at the view, trying not to think. I wish I had a book. Reading fills up my head so that I don't have to think. I'm getting up the courage to ask her if she has a book I can borrow when she speaks out of nowhere.

"My father was a trader. He always had a box of old books with his things. I liked the smell."

I nod, not wanting to break the spell by making any sound, but it's over anyway. Shirr drains her cup and places it back on the control panel with a small click.

I don't like the smell of old books, that musty vanilla tang.

Once, when I was lost in the twists and turns of a packed bookstall, an older man approached me. He had shadowed eyes that glowed red where the white should be. In the temple, they might have said that his *ether* was tainted, but I thought maybe he chewed yetta, a mind-altering stimulant that was part of the culture of certain planets and moons in the Hinga belt. It made his teeth black and his eyes blaze.

"You're such a pretty girl. How old are you?" he said, coming closer, too close. I shrank back into the books as his eyes ate me up. It was almost like he could taste my vulnerability, my aloneness. The stink of old paper and binding glue was overwhelming as he came closer. I was cornered, pressing into the stack of books at my back so hard, wishing I could go further and disappear into them. *Eat me up, books, before he does.* They didn't. His hands were clammy. They left skims of sweat on my arms, my thighs.

I have never liked the smell of old books, but I don't tell Shirr that. I don't want to ruin the moment.

"Do you want to tell me what happened?" Shirr says.

I've been waiting for her to ask, but not sure if she would. I've been dreading it. Everything in me wants to slide off the panel and retreat to somewhere quiet, not have to think about it or talk about it, but she's asked now. Fuck.

"I hitched a ride with a man," I say, slow, trying to phrase it just so, just enough and nothing more. "He attacked me. It happens."

She nods, her breath leaving her body in a huff that jets steam out of her nose in the cold air. "Happened before, has it?"

"Yeah. Not like that, but it's happened." I pause, and then add, "I don't want to talk about it."

She nods and is silent for a while, and I sit there, uncomfortable in the echo of it.

"I have a question for you," she says, but she doesn't ask it.

Instead, she walks off down the hall, and I'm not sure if I'm supposed to follow her, but then she turns and beckons. I slip off the control panel, the softness of my thighs scraping against the cold steel edge.

Shirr stops at the door between our bedrooms. Her hand is on the lever, but she doesn't flip it right away and waits for me to catch up. It's kind of like docking with her ship all over again. My mind jumps over possibilities: a collection of costumes that I'll have to wear for her amusement? Her collection of hitcher-bitch skulls? It could be anything.

It's not anything, though. It is something very specific. Something that I cannot say no to.

When she opens the door, the small room is completely lined with shelves, and each of the shelves is lined; they heap on piles on the floor, surrounding a chair that is soft and worn and makes me think of the word *home*, even though no home of mine has ever been soft like that.

Books. The room is full of books.

"Would you like to stay here?"

[2]

I remember every route we take by what I am reading.

In the long months between Normandy and Qīngtíng, in between my new duties on the ship, I pore over the collected works of Charles Dickens, JG Ballard, and Nnedi Okorafor. When we take a long ride through the Arcadias on a five-stop haul, I go deep into the contemporary philosopher Yasmin Maturo's books and reconceptualize my place in the galaxy. As we scattershoot across the ALLCorp Group doing short-run live export deliveries, I get into artificial speciation horror and beg Shirr never to haul livestock again.

I take whatever I'm reading down to the big, fancy holds on our rare cryo passenger runs, doing welfare and maintenance checks. I drift through the pod maze, a book held up as I move amongst gently glowing orbs with naked and floating passengers inside. It is no place for ghost stories. I almost give myself a heart attack reading Stephen King's *It* amongst the spectral forms in the half-light. Painted faces and imagined spiders linger in every shadowy corner.

She shows me how to do basic repairs on the ship. We spend hours in the engine bay, sweating over the routine maintenance. Shirr doesn't fuck around; she cares for her ship. The engine room is as pristine as the rest of *The Algea*, and she teaches me how to keep it that way. I learn to use the lifters, help load and unload. I like the work, the simplicity of mundane tasks, of working with my body.

Before Shirr and I sleep, we read books in the quiet. Sometimes, the loudest sound for hours is the clink of a teacup into a saucer.

When I wake screaming in the night, Shirr is always there to hold me and bring me back to myself. We fall asleep in my narrow bed, wake curled against each other.

When we deliver our cargo, I only leave the ship if I have to and count the hours before we're back in the endless black. I want to stay in the dark silence of space, in the *here but not here* fold of warp speed—invisible, impossible to find.

I never want to live another way again. I think maybe that I am happy.

And I let myself get used to things being good.

I should know better.

We see the body on Lozano in a tumbled pile of garbage spilling out of a dumpster at the dock. The piles of discarded plastic and rotting organics form a pyramid around the dumpster, and the body slumps on the plane of it, splayed and only slightly set back from the thoroughfare. I don't know why I go closer, because I don't want to see. Shirr doesn't say anything, and I look everywhere but at the body, like taking in the scene around her might make the bird-flutter of my heart stop. Trash blooms everywhere, flowering in the tropical heat, the stink of it nearly sweet.

There, next to the cheek, a tiny plastic robot fading in the sun.

By the foot, two empty kava bottles and a cat's skull. The crowd jostles us, and Shirr has to steady me because I think I'm going to fall over. My knees are hot and weak, my head spinning. The Force arrives and pushes everyone back.

The silver blanket catches the light as they spread it out over the body, blinding me for a moment. I can breathe again once she's been covered. I can almost breathe again.

The crowd sighs and jeers as the blanket obscures their view. I quake. This is not entertainment for me. A Force officer in their stiff blue uniform is rolling out tape to block the scene while two others supervise them. They laugh and joke as the red tape wraps around whatever will hold it up.

"Dunno why they didn't just blast her out the airlock before reentry," they say, and the onlookers all chortle, *ho ho ho*. "Save us the trouble."

"The person who did this wanted us to see the body," Shirr murmurs, and I can just hear her over the small crowd jostling for a look.

"Us?" I ask, feeling the cold fear curdle my blood, my guts. *Shick.*

She puts a rough, warm hand on my arm. "Not *us* specifically. Just anyone. To show their power, how this person is only visible now that they have made them visible."

Visible. Invisible. Were they like me? Fuck, did I know them? What were they like? What was their name?

Hitchers are so often loners by nature, because every single one of us is running from something. You don't live like this unless you have something to keep moving away from. Some of us know each other by sight, but we rarely mix, and when we do, it's always fleeting.

A memory spills out: spending four days with a silent hitcher about my age, their sweet-oiled dreadlocks spilling across my face as we fucked. We ate what we could scrounge and slept together behind a dumpster in Porti on Masa. Two was better than one to keep out the icy air on that cold planet. They didn't tell me their name. I didn't tell them mine. We parted when they got a ride, and I never saw them again.

That dumpster was a lot like this one.

I don't want to think about that. I try to put it away. It's so hard. It's too hard. I'm getting tired of folding up all the little boxes I put these things inside.

Shirr has noticed my discomfort. "I'm sorry, Evey, I should know better." She takes my arm to lead me away, but I flinch as she touches me. She looks hurt for a moment, but it barely registers. I can feel myself numbing to everything, a rapid decompression where all the hurt and fear drain out and leave me empty. I follow as Shirr weaves through the still-gathering crowd. I blink, seeing their faces like masks. Nothing feels real or right.

When we'd landed here, there was a notice about a worker strike at the dock, and garbage blooms from cans and bags into the street. I'm seeing limbs in every jumble of waste, lifeless faces in the piles that spill from every corner. I accidentally knock into a person carrying a massive load wrapped in tight black plastic on their head, and they scream at me in a language I don't understand as they struggle to keep their balance.

"Evey, are you okay?" Shir asks, pulling me away from them.

"I don't know," I tell her. I can barely feel my feet on the ground. Shirr stops me, kicks a bag of trash out of the gutter to make room, and makes me sit down with my head between my knees.

"Take deep breaths," she says. "I should have gotten you out of there sooner, I'm sorry."

It's hard, because the stink is horrific, but I do as she says and start to feel more grounded. I can feel my heart hammering in my chest, but as I breathe, it begins to slow. Finally, I look up. I can't meet her eyes, so I look past her to the people threading through the street, trying to focus on something.

"Thank—" I start to say, but the end of it dries up on my tongue.

Out of the overcast gloom, a face turns, the planes of it

changing, shifting into a form I recognize. A furrowed brow, cold smile. Eyes as black as the space between stars.

I shoot backward, scuttling in the refuse, trying to run, but my muscles are soup, and my bones are hot noodles, and I can't get up. I'm saying, "No no no no no," and Shirr grabs me, thumbs digging hard into my bicep. I remember that feeling, and I try to fight her.

"Evey! What is it? What's wrong?" She asks, holding me as I thrash limply in her grasp.

"It's him," I say.

"Who?"

"Him!"

"Where?" she asks. I search the faces, but there's only the shuffle of people passing—porters, loaders, traders with goats. Two people dressed in revealing finery, giggling to each other and throwing off sultry looks at passersby. A little bundle of street kids go by, calling and shouting. Their laughter echoes through my head.

"He was there," I tell her, and I can see her doubt, but she doesn't say a word.

I'm shaking, dread churning in my gut. I know I'm safe back on *The Algea*, but my body still thinks he's on the other side of the wall. I touch the cold surface to try and place myself. *You are here, safe.* Then it's like I almost hear the sound of him hammering on the other side, and I pull my hand away like it suddenly got hot.

"I don't want to dismiss your reality," Shirr says, handing me a cup of tea. "But you'd just had a shock. Seeing that body, it must have been hard. Are you sure it was him?"

"I could never forget his face," I say, blowing steam off the top of the cup.

Shirr nods. "Do you think it could have been a flashback?"

I stop mid-sip. I know it was his face, but was I seeing

something that was actually there? Or was his face a splash my brain painted, still in horror from seeing the person dead in the trash? I'd had flashbacks before, wild moments where it felt like I was living through the fear and pain again, and my body flooded with sick, hot terror. I'd seen and felt things long past but so real in the moment, and I started to doubt as well.

"Maybe," I say. I want it not to have been him. I want it to be my mind throwing up shades. I tell myself that it wasn't real. That he's gone. He's halfway across the galaxy, he's on the other side of the universe, he's in another dimension, he was sucked into a black hole. I try to gather the memories of his face together, box them up. I picture myself blasting it out of the airlock. Sometimes that helps.

***

Even though I've done it hundreds of times, and Shirr probably thousands, launch never ceases to set my heart pounding and frees a swarm of pollinator bots in my stomach. Once you're going fast in space, it doesn't feel like anything, but lift off feels like everything you've ever felt, multiplied by a million, and all at the same time.

I love being in space. I hate getting there.

We're right-angled to the ground, hanging inside by the grav panels, the hitch on our ship cradling the giant cargo bays. Two huge boosters clang into position, and the bots scurry down the cranes to fix them in place. My breathing is shallow and fast as the ship creaks and groans with the weight. Shirr fusses with the launch sequence, mumbling to herself like she always does. I cinch the straps across my chest tight, tighter, tightest.

"One minute to launch," comes across the comms from the flight control, and Shirr gives the okay. The countdown flashes on the view. As the numbers click down, I close my eyes and concentrate on my breath, trying to make it deep and slow. When the counter hits single digits, my body flows with adrenaline, heart slamming hard.

With ignition, *The Algea* shudders, and everything suddenly becomes a roar that envelopes the whole world. My chest clenches, and I hold my breath even though I'm trying hard not to. The ship rises slow-then-fast, the whole thing shaking, threatening to tear itself to pieces. I'm never as aware of how fragile the ship is until ignition and gravity battle between lifting us up and keeping us on the ground. I can't help but wail as the sound splits everything apart inside me, but I can't even hear myself do it, just feel it rising up out of my throat, quaking with the tremble of the ship. I'm sucked back hard in my seat, the Gs holding me tight there, driving my body back. I feel so small, so fucking fragile. My body was not meant for this, not meant to bear these forces.

If I wanted to open my eyes, I could watch the sky go blue-white-black in the view, but I keep them closed. I know what it looks like. The first few times it's beautiful. Now it's just land, then sky, then black.

I could try to enjoy it. It's inevitable: What comes down must go back up again. But I can't help my fear response; my body is primed in fight-or-flight at all times. I am always bracing.

Launch is something scarier than a thought or a memory. It's something real and whole to be afraid of; fire, decompression, mid-air break-apart. My soft body torn apart by forces too big and fast to even see, only feel. Fire and flames and melting steel. I let my body feel this fear; this fear is natural. It's healthy.

I slam the book I'm reading onto the dining table, making all the plates and cups jump. Shirr comes running in from the bridge where she'd been poring over charts and plotting courses for our next multi-run contract.

"What's wrong?" she asks.

"Too many dead girls," I say.

She glances at the book's cover, face-up amongst the dinner

things I was supposed to be clearing away. It's a tattered murder mystery, pages warped and yellowed, the spine cracked so much the title is barely visible.

"Evey, why do you read these things?"

"I don't know," I tell her, standing to fill the kettle. I take our cups, neatly rinsed and dried by the sink, and I fill two strainers with leaves. "Every one of these that I read, it's always a dead girl. It's like a game to play, solve this puzzle. But it's almost always a woman, and she's always dead. That's not a puzzle; it's not entertainment. It's a tragedy."

"Yes!" she says, throwing up her hands. "Which is why I can't understand why you would want to read this shit. I read to relax and escape, or to learn something. I don't read to torment myself."

The kettle clicks off, steam rising off the almost-boiling water. I pour it into the pot, and the smell of fragrant jasmine tea fills the kitchen. I pour out my own cup after a minute, so it doesn't taste bitter, but Shirr likes it stronger, so I let the leaves steep before I pour hers.

"It's not as if they don't hurt me," I say, slowly. "They do. But they make me feel . . . safe, too. That's not the right word, exactly, but it's close."

Shirr blows on the cup I hand to her. "After what you've been through . . . I don't know how you can do it to yourself. Isn't it like pouring acid on a wound?"

"A little. But it's like I can't look away, to the point that I start to seek it out," I tell her. "Even though it's painful. Maybe it's some kind of masochism?"

"I don't think I could bear it. Not after what I've . . . and you ..." She hesitates like she's weighing her experiences against mine, like she's doing the maths on pain and fear and memory. Is $a + b > c$? Are my hurts worth the same as yours? She is quiet for a while before she speaks again.

"I've not said it before, but I want you to know how strong I think you are."

"This isn't about my books anymore," I say.

"No, it's not. I know you prefer not to talk about it, and I don't want to ask you to. But maybe it would help if you did."

"Do you want to hear it?" I ask.

"Only if you want to tell me," she says.

For a moment, I picture the memories I keep, filed away in their little boxes. I imagine taking them down one by one, opening them for her. The ones that hold all my hurts, my fear. Memories of the temple, the priests, incense, and altars. The one that holds *him*, and the memories of those long hours on his ship, the pain and indignity.

But she has done it for me. I can do it for her.

"I don't want to go into detail."

"You don't have to. I don't need to know everything he did to you," she says. "I don't want gratuitous description; I don't need you to fill in those blanks. You know I've got an idea of what people are capable of."

"Then what? What do you want to know?" I ask.

"Maybe it would help to talk about how you felt. I . . . I think if you can give a name to those feelings, they aren't as potent. I'm not an expert on trauma, but I do know this: Hope dies in silence. You don't have to hold this on your own. I can take a little of the weight of it."

Shirr doesn't try to take my hand. Instead, she slides her hand across to me, palm up, offering it. I don't take it, but she doesn't move it away.

It takes me a long time to start talking, and when I do, my sentences come staggered. "Everything. He did. It was bad, yes. Yes. But the worst. The worst feeling. Was when he. When he changed. When his eyes. Went. Black." I can't look at Shirr, so I stare at the ground, my feet, the kettle still steaming, anywhere but her sympathetic face. As I go on, the words come easier. "I felt so stupid. For a minute, I felt like . . . This is what you get, Evey. This is what you get for being stupid, for putting yourself in this position. And then the dread. The dread, Shirr. It was almost better after. Almost, because I knew what I was in for."

"You didn't deserve what happened because you made a mistake. Do you know that?"

"I do, yes." I'm shaking. "But it's hard to really believe it."

"I know," she says, and I know she does. I reach out and take her hand. It is dry and rough, steady.

"Thank you for trusting me, Evey."

"Thank you for making me feel like I can trust you," I tell her.

***

"I loved it out here," I tell Shirr. I'm perched on my little clear spot on the control panel, face pressed against the viewport, watching the stars bend around the warp bubble.

"The Pearl Galaxy?" Shirr asks, looking up from her navigation charts.

"No, not here exactly," I say. "I just mean, I loved being in space."

"Why do you use the past tense?"

"You know why," I tell her. "He ruined it."

Shirr puts her screen down. "Tea?"

"Yes, please."

I climb off my spot on the control panel and pad down the shadowed hallway after Shirr in my bare feet. The cold of the steel floor comes through the threadbare rug that runs the length of the hallway, but I ignore it. In the kitchen, she fills two cups with boiling water from the kettle and measures out some Assam tea. Shirr knows just how I like it, with twice as much soy milk as she takes and a teaspoon of sugar. She sometimes calls me uncouth for taking so much sugar in my tea, and I always tell her to stop being so Spartan.

"You still love it out here," Shirr says, taking a seat and placing my cup in front of me. "It's still under there, behind the fear." She touches me gently on the chest, fingers tapping lightly on my breastbone. I like the familiarity of her touch, the warmth of her fingertips on my cool skin. "Why? What do you love about being in space?"

"Everything," I say. "The view. I like looking out on it and thinking about the universe. About distance and time, relativity. I like the quiet most of all. Growing up, there were always bells ringing. Those fucking bells! And the sound of the acolytes praying in shifts was this constant hum just above the level where you can ignore it. I didn't hear silence until I was in space that first time. It made my head feel peaceful. After my first trip, I knew I wanted to stay out here."

I almost tell her about how being in warp makes me feel like I don't exist, or like I don't have to exist, but I don't. I'm not sure she will understand. I barely understand.

"Do you think that might be part of why you chose to live the way you did?" She asks. "Hitching rides, I mean. Because you love being off-planet?"

"Yes, I think that was part of it. It's one way to get up here."

We sit and sip our tea quietly. Neither of us feels the need to fill the silence right away. We sit companionably for a while until I get the urge to speak, to give her something of myself.

"When he had me, and when I escaped in the pod . . . it's almost like he used everything I love about being in space against me. The vastness, the silence, the elasticity of time. I've always felt small out here, but it felt miraculous that I existed at all. On his ship, in that pod, I felt so tiny and insignificant. It made me realize that I don't matter, not at all."

"You do matter," she says, and I nod because she's right, but she's also wrong.

"People matter to different degrees," I say. "It depends on the context. In there, then, I didn't matter. I had the same significance as a speck of dust. I can't ever forget what it feels like."

"I'm sorry. I hate that you felt that way."

"I could be happy here, though," I say. I'd been frightened to say the words, like letting anyone know what this life meant to me might spoil it in some way, as if naming it meant it could be snatched away. "I could heal here, I think."

"I think you can," Shirr says. "I have."

I don't ask, and she doesn't elaborate. I tell myself we have time.

Xiàtiān is in its spring, and the air is warm on my bare arms. Sitting high up on one of *The Algea's* open hatches, I'm gently swinging my legs off the edge, a book resting on my lap. It's a good place to read up here, out in the fresh air but unnoticed in the busy dockland because I'm so high up. There's enough to see at eye level that no one thinks to look up, and I like the anonymity of being above eyeline. I lift my head to Xiàtiān's sun, feeling the gentle heat of it and the cool breeze play across my skin. The docks are dirty and busy, like docks always are, but in the distance, I can see mountains. They gleam purple in the morning haze, dense with vegetation. I ache to be able to go to them, to be able to leave the docks and move around freely, instead of being stuck amongst the ships and loading bays for lack of documentation. I try to imagine what a forest might be like. I imagine they are deliciously cool, shaded, and quiet.

Then I see him. It's not like when I saw him on Lozano, when the world slowed, and everything went dark except his face. This time, he simply passes by, just some guy carrying a sack of rice on one shoulder and a sack of potatoes on the other. But it is unmistakably him, the same rough features of his face, the wiry body, the quick, long stride. I don't jump or scream or run. I freeze, my book falling out of my lap and thumping onto the dirt below the open hatch. He doesn't notice.

he isn't real, it's not real, that's not him

But I know what my eyes are seeing, and I know how hard my

heart is beating. I tell myself again that I'm just mad, I'm seeing things, this is just my mind throwing out a glitch from the damage he did. It's just someone who looks like him or walks like him, and I've woven it into something else. I close my eyes and count to ten, and when I open them, he is gone.

see? he is gone. he is gone because he was never there.

I'm still staring at the place where he was when Shirr calls up to me.

"Evey, are you okay?" She picks up my book, dusts it off, and holds it up to me. "You dropped this."

"I'm fine!" I yell down to her. She opens the loading bay, and I close the upper hatch, padding through the passageways with my bare feet on cool steel. We meet in the kitchen. My book is on the table, battered and dirty, some of the pages rumpled. I touch it, thinking of him. Trying not to think of him.

"Are you okay?" Shirr asks me. "Did something happen?"

Even though I mean to tell her, what comes out instead is, "No." It doesn't feel like a lie, because if what I saw isn't real, then it doesn't count. If it is real, then he is *here*, and how can he be? Space is too infinite, and we are too small. The thought that he could have passed only meters below my bare, swinging feet makes me feel so sick with fear that I close the possibility off, box it up. Eject it out into space. I'm seeing things, having flashbacks, am losing my mind. Madness is preferable to the possibility that I could feel his cold hands on me again.

I touch the battered book on the table. "I lost my place."

"You'll find it again," Shirr says, but I know I'll never read another word.

———

His face begins to haunt me. It's not a dream specter, I see him when I'm awake. I see his face in crowds on Seba and J-6. He passes me one night as we leave a market on Efa. When we're loading up the cargo holds at the Precipice City docks on Plano, I catch a glimpse of him in the corner of my eye and clip the loading hatch with the hauler. I can't stop shaking for hours.

When we're docked, all I can think about is being back in warp, far away from the crowded docks and the faces that could suddenly become his. The wounds inside me get to knit in the long months between landfalls, but they tear open again when we're back on solid soil. Fear drags me down like heavy gravity.

I wish we could cruise through space without end, no need to re-up fuel, no deadlines or deliveries. Just me and Shirr on the ship in our quiet bubble of space and time, hurtling through space as we put light-years between us and anywhere he might be.

I hide it from Shirr, but she can feel it in the air between us, the way my mood moves against hers in the small space of the ship.

"Something's wrong," she says one night when we're in the library. It's not a question; she is not asking me if something is wrong, she's telling me.

"I'm fine," I say, but Shirr's question jars me, like I've been shaken out of sleep. I feel half in the room, half out of it, and her words have me scrambling back into myself.

"Evey, you've been reaching for that book for the last ten minutes."

"What?" I ask. Now that she's said it, I can see that she is right. My hand is brushing the spine of a book on a shelf at eye level. I let it drop.

"You've just been *standing there*," Shirr says, and her voice is at the edge of cracking.

"I'm okay," I lie. I don't know why I haven't been able to tell her, why the words keep getting lost between my brain and mouth.

"What is it?" Shirr asks, rising and coming over. She reaches for my hand, and I flinch. Hurt flares in her face, and I rinse through with shame because I know she would never hurt me. "What aren't you telling me?"

I perch on the edge of the chair, trying to say the words. I count down: three, two, one, *speak*. Nothing comes. I try again, still no words. I know I can say anything to her, know she won't judge me or think I'm mad, but as much as I know that, there's still a fear gripping my vocal cords like a firm hand on my throat. Speaking makes things real. Telling the story gives it a shape, a body. Once you've said something, it is so much harder to box it up and pack it away, to forget, forget, forget. I look out through the viewport and imagine blasting all those bundles out of the airlock. All my worst memories, floating frozen through space forever, further and further away.

"I'll be back," Shirr says, and I'm so wrapped up in untangling the words knotted in my mouth that I barely notice the time pass. In what feels like moments, she's pressing a hot cup of dark Assam tea into my hands. The gentle burn of the cup helps to bring me back into myself.

"Can I tell you a story?" Shirr asks, and I nod, sipping the tea even though I know it's too hot. The burning liquid is sweet, and it sears down my throat. Still unable to speak, I just bob my head up and down. She sits on the floor in front of me, stretching out her long legs in front of her and placing her own cup down on the rug.

"It's about how I ended up with *The Algea*." I'm staring at her feet, bare, the toes long and dusted with a few fine hairs, but when she speaks, I look up at her face.

"She wasn't always mine," she says. "Of course. But I didn't buy her, I inherited the ship. In a way. *The Algea* belonged to my mother, and her mother before that. She died when I was seventeen. My father—" she pauses for a fraction of a second, just a tiny trip, a little crack in her voice. "My father killed her. She told him over and over that he'd end up killing her one day, and one day he did."

I don't know what to say, in a different way from my silence before. But I don't think Shirr wants me to say anything.

"He took the ship once she was dead, and there was nowhere else to go, so I stayed with him. I didn't know anything else. I thought it was normal for a father to hit his partner, his child . . . Anyway, once she was gone, I got all of his rage instead of her." Shirr pauses, lifts her cup, and takes a sip. Little twirls of steam play across the top of the cup. She tells the story easily, but somehow, I know she hasn't told anyone else before. It carries the weight of something held close, buried down, boxed up.

"One night, he started beating me, and I fought back. It hadn't occurred to me to ever fight back, maybe because my mother never did, but this time I did. Maybe it was because I was already black and blue from the night before, or maybe I was just done. I gave him everything I had."

I don't know why I feel like I need to be close to her, but I do. I slide out of my chair and sit next to her on the rug. She reaches out for my hand.

"He laughed at me at first, but when he saw I wasn't playing, it got serious. After a while, I stopped being able to fight back. I was almost senseless. That's when I saw the pliers. They were needle-nose, not really sharp, but pointed, and they were close enough to reach. So, I did."

She knows that I know what she's going to say, so she doesn't need to form it into words.

"Afterward, I cleaned the blood up and put his body in the airlock. I didn't want to watch it go, but I did. He will be floating out there forever, which is what he deserves."

Shirr doesn't say anything more. There's no lesson to be learned from this story, it's just that, a story. An offering to me so that I know I'm safe to tell her anything. But the telling has touched something in her, and she curls up, her head in my lap. I run my fingers through her shorn, greying hair, the stiff spikes of it feeling nice under my fingertips. We sit like that for a while, letting the silence press all around us.

"I keep seeing him, Shirr," I finally say. She sits up.

"Where?"

"Plano, Seba, Efa. Here. All the ports we've called at. I see his face in crowds, in passing. I think I'm losing my mind."

Shirr wraps her arms around me. "You're not, Evey," she says into my shoulder, voice muffled into my coverall. "You've been through so much. It's a natural response to trauma."

"I know," I say, my voice muffled in her neck, too. "But every time I think I'm starting to feel better, boom, there he is again. It feels so real. I saw him pass me yesterday carrying supplies. And once steering a loader. It's not like he's lurking in the shadows or lunging at me in the dark. It's just so . . . normal. But it can't be real, how could it be? How could he be everywhere that we are? It's stupid, it doesn't make sense."

Shirr sits up fast, knocking over her cup, the milky tea splashing puddles and droplets across the rug that sink fast into the fibers, turning them dark.

"But it does make sense!" She says, jumping up and rushing to the bridge. I scramble to my feet and follow. Shirr's on her tablet, scrolling through files, and finally, she finds what she's looking for. She thrusts it into my face, and the letters scramble on the screen as I try to focus.

"What is this?"

"It's our contract for this series of deliveries."

"So? What does that have to do with—?"

"It's rare that we're the only hauler doing these jobs. There are usually tens, even hundreds of ships doing the same trips for the same corporations."

"You think he's . . ."

"I think he's on the same contract as us. It would make sense, given the route I found you on."

I collapse into her arms, the world feeling suddenly so cold around me, but her body pressing into mine is warm and whole and breathing and alive.

"I don't think you're losing your mind, Evey. I think it's really him."

And I shudder into her because I'm suddenly not sure what's worse.

When I close my eyes, I see myself floating in the lifepod. It's like I'm looking at myself from a long way away, and I'm not dead or alive but something else, hovering in a space between yes and no, up and down, life and death.

I don't want to think about it.

I want to go back into the library and keep reading the book on fractal engineering that I'm halfway through. I want to get in the shower and waste a bunch of fuel recycling a torrent of hot water that I can use to scrub away the memory of the murdered girl, the lifepod, the *shick* and shiver of a knife at my throat.

I want to obliterate myself and find a way to forget my entire life.

In the middle of the sleep cycle, I untangle myself from Shirr's warm arms and walk down to the bridge, bare feet padding on the rug. I find her hand unit, which has set itself to sleep in the night, wake it, and head to the kitchen. I perch at the table, searching the port manifest. Scrolling through hundreds of ships, dates, numbers, my eyes tear up from tiredness, and all the names begin to blur. I'm ready to give up when I see it. It stands out amongst the others, stark, the pixels seeming sharper, more jagged than the others.

"Shirr?" I call out, my voice turning to dust and my heart jump-jumping in its shroud of bone and muscle. A vision of the blocky letters painted next to the hatch jumps into my mind's eye. Shirr comes running but stops when she sees me sitting calmly at the kitchen table.

"Here, look." I pass her the hand unit, and she takes it, blinking in the light, and switching the kettle on.

"Halfway down. *Boş.* Class C cargo hauler." My words don't sound like mine, flat and quiet and droning. "I think that's it." I remember the cedilla below the 's' and knew it was a class C by the sight of it.

"Looks like he'll land on Vica twenty-six hours before we do," she says.

I wish we didn't have to go to Vica. I wish we could jettison the cargo, take off into warp, and never come out. I stare at the tabletop, losing time until Shirr puts her hand on my shoulder.

"Are you there, Evey?"

I nod. A question jumps into my mind, and I say it with no pause between to even think.

"Why did you stop for me?" I know I don't need to explain further; she knows what I mean, and she's not surprised by the question, like maybe she's been waiting for me to ask it.

She doesn't say anything for a bit, pulling out the things for tea, silent until she comes back with the steaming cups. She watches me take the first sip, and then she starts to talk.

"When I saw your lifepod signal, I was so close to coding it in as an error. I didn't want to have to stop for no reason. But the signal was in the middle of so much nothing that it made me feel sick. I came out of warp without even realizing I was making the command. Then I saw you, saw the state you were in, and I felt sicker because I nearly left you to die like that."

I nod, keeping silent. She doesn't want my thanks or for me to even say anything. She's not done.

"*He* did that to you," she says, the emphasis on 'he' coming out in her voice. "So, we're going to find him. I can't bear the thought of that happening to someone else. Because no one else knows what he is, but we do. And if he does it again, it's on us now."

"No, it's on him. It's always on him," I say.

Shirr nods. "Yes, it's on him to choose not to kill. But he isn't choosing that. So, it's up to us to stop him. No one else knows. No one else cares."

"No one else will," I say, and I sound like I'm trying to convince myself.

She nods. "No one else will."

"Do you think he killed that person by the dumpster on Lozano?"

"Yes," Shirr says slowly. "I think he killed them. Lozano was the first stop on this contract; he was definitely there. But even if he didn't, he's killed many more. You must know that."

"The room, the room he kept me in, it had old blood on the floor, the walls." The memory twists my stomach, and I try to box the feeling up without success.

forget forget forget.

"How many?" Shirr asks. "How many do you think he's killed? How many didn't get away? And how many more will he kill if we don't do something?"

I want to vomit, scream, run away. Anything.

"What will we do if we find him?" I ask. This is another question that has been hanging between us, unspoken.

She looks at me and says it with such simplicity that it startles me.

"We'll kill him."

"Oh," I say softly, even though I knew it in my guts all along.

$$[\ 3\ ]$$

We cut through the cloud, and the view of Vica clears in the front view. The atmosphere roars all around us, shocking after the silence of space. The planet is icy in its perpetual winter, crowded with great mountain crags, snow-capped, and growing closer. The main cargo port on the continent of Arcadia is in a city called First, and it takes us thirty minutes or so to descend. It exists in the shadow of a plateau a kilometer high and is cradled on the other side by a lower mountain. I've been here before. It's a fucker of a place. The only sun warms the city for a few hours a day before it's lost again, dipping behind the plateau's sheer face.

"I don't like this place," Shirr says, hands on the controls and eyes locked on the view, focused on steering *The Algea* and its massive cargo holds through the wind shear coming off the mountains. I'm strapped in, shaking and jolting as we hit air pockets, thermals, updrafts.

"I don't like it either," I tell her.

Then we're in sight of the dock, a grubby smear in the valley, crowded with haulers. Shirr steers us into our bay, and we lock in with a massive crunch.

"Have you been here before?" she asks, continuing our

conversation as we sit in the kitchen. She's chopping onions, and I'm rinsing rice for dinner. Outside we can hear the docking bots crawling over the cargo holds, unlocking the huge mineral storage units from our hauler. We're not needed for this part and for us, it's late.

"Twice. It's a hard place. The Force here are vicious. Have you ever been somewhere that just feels mean?"

"I think I have, yes."

I'm feeling open and words come easily for once. "Et is mean. Where I grew up. Everything is so sumptuous; the streets are actually paved in gold, but everyone there is as hard and cool as steel. The wealth gets into their hearts and makes them cold. It's like that here, too, like maybe the cold gets into people's hearts, makes it always winter there as well." I put the rice into the cooker and press the button, then join Shirr at the table, where I snip the tops and tails from large blue beans.

"The streets are paved with gold? Really? I thought that was just a tall tale."

"It's true. There's a lot of gold on Et, so much they don't need to sell all of it. It's so ostentatious. Everywhere you go, you just get blinded by it. It's ridiculous."

"And you left that," she says, throwing the onions into a pan of hot oil on the stove. It's not a question, because Shirr knows the answer to it.

"I left that. I gave that up to work cargo and turn tricks for lifts through the galaxies."

"It must have been hard," she says.

"It was, but it was better than what I'd watched my mother and the other acolytes go through at the hands of the priests. Better than what was waiting for me."

"What was waiting for you?" Shirr asks, and I can tell she thought carefully before asking. She doesn't look at me and instead drops pinches of this and that into the curry, the kitchen filling with the smell of spices, ginger, kimopt, and garlic.

I decide to answer. I know she won't mind either way, but I feel open with her, like it's okay to talk about horrible things as we make dinner, like the domesticity takes some of the hurt out of it. She has a way of doing that.

"Do you know what infibulation is?"

She stops her seasoning, dropping a packet of lablin leaf onto the floor.

"Shit, Evey. Genital mutilation?"

"I ran away when I started menstruating," I tell her, squatting down to help her pick up the leaves from the floor. She drops them into the food waste bin. "I saw what they left my mother with. That pain wasn't for me." I go to rise but remember the other pain that was waiting in my future, and my legs give way. I fall back onto my ass, and start to laugh, start to cry. Shirr offers me her hand, and I look up into her soft-lined face, her head haloed in the kitchen's yellow downlight.

"What is it with men and blades?" I ask her as she hauls me to my feet, still laughing, tears spilling down my face, voice cracking on the last word. She hugs me, and I let her, my arms stiff at my sides, all her questions dried up. She adds keyo milk to the curry, stirring as it thickens. The smell of the food is sweet, earthy. The click of the rice cooker turning off and the clacks of the bots on the hull are the only sounds that break the quiet.

Shirr serves. We eat. We don't say anything for a long time.

"How do we do this?" I say to Shirr, slipping a little on the frosted path, almost dropping the rolls of copper wire in my arms. I'm bundled in a coat, gloves, a hat, and the chill still bites me through them all. I remember being here before, trying to steal enough to keep myself warm, finding other dock lurkers and huddling with them for precious heat, ready to take a ride with anyone and do almost anything for it, just to escape the cold that seeped into my bones.

"I don't know, I've never done something like this before," Shirr says, taking one of the rolls out of my hands. "Last time . . . I was just acting on instinct."

"How does he do it? Do you think he's just acting on instinct, too?" I ask.

"Maybe. Or maybe it's deliberate. Maybe he hunts."

"He didn't have to hunt me," I tell her, as we arrive back at *The Algea,* and Shirr opens the hatch. I dump my armful onto the grate floor and flop down myself. "I approached *him.* I walked right up and asked him to take me off-planet all alone. What an idiot."

"You aren't an idiot," Shirr says, touching my shoulder gently as she passes me. She packs away the rolls of wire, fiber-optic cable, diamondbond, and all the other mechanical and repair supplies we picked up this morning, while I stare out of the hatch, watching the dock crowds go by, trying to box up all my shame. She comes to sit beside me.

"Making yourself open to vulnerable people is a kind of hunting, if that makes sense," she says, and I drop my head onto her shoulder, feeling the scratchiness of her kroll wool coat on my cheek, feeling the in and out of her breath as she talks.

"Kind of."

"No, it is. It's like how the defenseless sometimes give off a beacon to those who would take advantage of them. Maybe he's got something that calls them to him."

"I don't think he even needs to. I'm not sure you know how desperate people can get."

Shirr looks offended for a moment, but then her face softens because she knows I'm not trying to diminish her. "I feel like I can imagine."

"You can, but you can't, too. In a place like this, when you're cold deep in your blood, so hungry you feel sick, tired, but you can't sleep because the ground is wet . . . the misery is endless. The pain, it hurts so bad. It makes you willing to do anything, anything to escape it. They know that," I say, gesturing to the hatch, to the outside, to the nameless *they* who stalk these places, the hard places where the smell of desperation carries on the cold air. "They eat it up."

"Is that what we should do? Make ourselves vulnerable?" Shirr says, but we both know she means me. There aren't a lot of older hitchers. They either find a way to settle down, or they just disappear. The ones that persist are so distinctive, so wizened and withered and hard that they're like weathered steel. No one would think that Shirr, with her soft grey hair and soft hips, could be one of these gnarled travelers.

"No, it has to be me," I tell her, saying what she already knows.

"Yes," she says. "It does. If we do this, it will have to be you."

"What do you mean if? We're doing it. It's decided."

Shirr shakes her head. "No, it's not. We don't have to do anything. We can load the hauler, lift off early, get this contract done and forget about it. Live our lives. Read, fly, be together. All the things we love."

She says the love part not looking at me, and I look away from her, too, because she's never said anything like it, and I've never heard anything like it. It makes my heart soar, then bottom out. It feels wonderful and terrible and frightening and massive all at once.

"We can even break the contract. Find a new one, and there'll be almost no chance we'll ever see him again."

"No," I tell her. "We're doing this. It's . . . It's worth my life to save who knows how many more from death, and worse."

"Was what he did to you worse than death?" she asks.

I don't hesitate for a moment. "Yes."

"Do you wish you had died?"

I pause this time. If I had died, I wouldn't have met Shirr. Never known that life could be like this. Missed out on so many things: all the books I wouldn't have read, knowing what it felt like to sit around a table and make dinner while music plays and we both sing along, sleeping on a soft bed with my body curled around hers, looking out at the stars while she navigates, plotting courses quietly in the sweet fold of warp. The feeling of home, and hope, and like I have a future.

"No," I say. "And that's why we're doing this. The ones he takes, they deserve the chance to have what I have. If I have to be bait, then thread me on a hook."

They are big words, and I believe them in my heart. But I feel the fear rise. Words are easy to say, action is another thing altogether.

"What if he does it to you again, Evey?" Shirr asks. "What if that's the price?"

I look at her; she looks at me and touches my face.

"Then I hope it's quick this time," I tell her.

It takes everything I have inside me to step out of the shadows. My hands tremble, guts churn, legs go numb. I can barely feel the ground underneath my feet, like I'm walking on stilts high above the slick, wet road.

He arrived on Vica a day before we did, and it was easy enough to knock the ice from the screen of an infobooth by the dock market and find his assigned bay. I roughed myself up a bit, took off a few layers to make the ice in my bones obvious and genuine.

I'm not sure what will happen when he sees me. Will he blink, shocked to see me alive but hiding it under his stone gaze? Will he rush me with his blade, gutting me in the open, with no care for the witnesses who will watch in stunned disbelief as I bleed out on the frigid ground?

He doesn't, though. I'm not prepared for his reaction.

I step out of the cover of a market stall awning as he parks his loader, everything in me screaming to run, run, run. I feel Shirr's eyes on me, can feel her fear creeping through my every jumpy nerve along with my own as she waits in the shadows, armed with a blaster holstered at her waist, her hand trembling and poised over it.

He steps down from the cab of his old loader, the dark green paint chipped in places and worn around the joins. He lifts his face toward me, and I'm sure it's at a regular speed, but to me, it happens in super slow motion, every plane and angle changing in the cool light. Blood rushes in my ears, roaring like an engine, until his cold eyes meet mine, and I wait for the recognition, the reaction, the jump. I wait for his face to twist, his body to tense, his hand to go for his knife.

It does not come.

'Yes?" he asks, wiping his hands on the grimy legs of his coverall. His voice is calm, even, almost pleasant. "Can I help you with something?"

Everything crashes down inside me and all around. It feels like the earth shakes, like all the walls fall, the ships tip and thunder to the ground. It feels like lift off times a million, times a billion, because this man, this man who almost took my life, who guided me through the very barest core of myself with a blade, revealed my smallness to me, my utter insignificance, and left me to die in indignity and foulness—

He does not recognize me. He doesn't know who I am.

"No," I say, and the voice that comes out of me is cool and calm and as icy as the bare, scraped earth of the plateau that stretches high above this city in the valley. "I thought you were someone else."

———

"Talk to me, Evey," Shirr says, worrying around me, her movements jagged and fraught. I'm sitting cross-legged on the floor of the empty loading bay, my head a nightmare.

"I'm thinking," I tell her. "I'm trying not to think."

She pauses in her nervous back and forth. "What about?" she asks, her face a twist of concern, and I want to reassure her that I'm okay, but in my head and my chest, I feel as cold as the frigid winds that scrape the cliffs around the city.

"About him killing me," I say. "About me killing him."

"Okay," she says, slowly. I don't look at her, can't. I keep staring at the curving steel walls of the loading bay, counting the rivets in the seams. "What happened? Please tell me what happened. He spoke to you. What did he say? Why did you run back here so fast? Why didn't you wait for me?"

Her hand touches my shoulder, and it brings me back into myself a little, but I don't want to be back in myself because if I am, I'm going to have to feel it, feel just how insignificant I am, how fucking *forgettable*. I'm trying to contain it, to make the boxes this pain can fit inside, but I don't have anything big enough to hold this agony. I want to pierce my skull, let the hurt suck out like air through a hull breach.

Shirr sits in front of me, cross-legged, mirroring my posture. Her knees touch mine, her face harsh-lit, each line around her mouth and eyes carved deep by the cool loading bay light. She takes my hand in both of hers. "Talk to me, Evey. Please. Please remember that the only thing that's ever helped to stop the hurt is sharing it. You can say anything to me, I'll listen. I won't ever turn away from you. Even if it's horrible. This shit thrives in silence."

I fling her hands away from mine, push back from her, spring up. "It's not horrible! It's not anything!" I kick at a lifting trolley, and it clatters away, slamming into the wall with a clang that echoes around the loading bay.

Shirr waits for the silence to fall again. "What do you mean it's not anything?"

"He didn't remember me!" I scream, and it bounces off the walls, too, just like it's been echoing around my head. "Why does that hurt so much? Fuck!"

The pain comes out of me in waves, and I can't control my body. I hit myself, careen into the walls, grab handfuls of my hair, wail until I can't catch my breath. Sucking in great, grating lungfuls, I still can't get enough air. Shirr watches as I try to wring myself out, try to take a breath. I see her face in flashes, almost kind, and when things start to go black around the edges, I feel her catch me. I'm in her arms, we're on the stairs, she's peeling my coverall off. Warmth cascades down my body, and she murmurs things I can't quite hear over the sound of the shower. The water wakes me, grounds me, and brings me back into myself, even though I'm not entirely sure I want to be here.

"Am I so forgettable?" I ask her, touching my arms, my legs, my face to make sure I am real.

"I remember you," Shirr says over the patter of the water onto the tiles.

———

The *shick* brings me out of sleep like it has so many nights before. My hair is bunched in wet tangles on the pillow, and I can feel the damp fabric beneath my cheek. I flip the pillow with heavy arms, the ache in my body magnified in the bruises I can feel blooming in the places where my soft flesh met the hard steel.

"Don't scream, Evey," Shirr says.

"What?"

I reach for the light and flick it on. The tableau before me is something I've felt but never seen, and it's more awful to witness than I could have imagined. He is here, on *The Algea*, in Shirr's bedroom. He looks like a tear in reality, like something completely incongruous. And he has Shirr, he has her, his hand around her throat and the knife

shick

tip digging into the soft skin just beneath her eye, a small droplet of blood beginning to bead there.

"You . . . you didn't remember me," I say, knowing how stupid it sounds, but fear makes me stupid, and he is the thing I am the most afraid of.

"I remembered you. You got away, of course I remember." He looks right at me, into me, strips me bare with his gaze, flays me, twists my guts, and hammers my heart. "I remember all my girls."

"They aren't your girls," Shirr says, and he drops the hand with the knife in it and kicks at the back of her knee, which makes her fall forward. It's been a while since she buzzed her head, and he has just enough hair to hold. He wrenches her up by it, and the knife goes to her throat.

"Nothing you say matters, you old bitch."

I cry out.

He marches Shirr out of the room, and I follow at their heels, begging him. "Please don't hurt her, don't hurt her, please . . ." I'm grabbing at him like I have the strength to pry him off her, which I know I don't.

He still has Shirr by the hair, but he lashes out with his other arm. His elbow smacks into the side of my face, and I feel my jaw rock. Everything goes grey and slow. Black creeps around the edges as I fall, and the last thing I see is his boots and Shirr's bare feet moving away from me. Then everything goes white.

[4]

I wake calling Shirr's name. At first, I don't know why I'm saying it, and it takes me more than a few minutes to remember. When I do, it rushes in—him, the horror, his knife beading blood under Shirr's eye. I stumble around looking for them, but I know it's been a long time since he knocked me out, hours at least, when I catch a glimpse of myself in the small mirror in the bathroom. My jaw is swollen, and deep purple bruises are already blooming across my cheek and spilling across my neck and ear. I touch the bruises firmly, letting the hurt wake me up, sharpen my focus.

From the bridge, I take Shirr's hand unit and download the latest port manifest. I know what I'm looking for this time, searching for the familiar name of his ship. *Boş*. A little noise comes out of my mouth, a sound so small compared to the great grip on my chest that tightens when I see that his ship was slated to leave an hour and a half ago, and it did not miss its window. He is gone. And Shirr is with him. My mind spins, all the boxes of forgetting that I've kept locked up tight now spill open, and I'm flooded with the memories of every moment of fear and pain under his empty gaze, deluged by the knowledge that it waits for Shirr, too.

no no no no

not her not her

I can only think of one thing to do.

The Algea is silent, void. The only sounds are my footsteps, the dull thud of my feet on the long, thin rugs that run through the halls of the living quarters. I dress, grabbing the first coverall I can find, slip on socks and boots, and hunt desperately for my coat. My breath is ragged by the time I find it. The thump of my heavy boots clattering down the grated metal stairs toward the cargo bay echoes through the emptiness of the ship.

The long Vica night is in its dying hours, and the hatch opens to an almost deserted dockland. I run from pool to pool of the bright white light that spills from every docked ship, stepping now and then into the orange glow of the dock lamps swinging from tall poles here and there. The only movement is the scurry of bots joining cargo holds to haulers. Every warm-blooded creature is hidden away from the frigid night, and I shudder when I think of Shirr and her bare feet on the frozen ground. I remember trying to keep warm here on my first visit, the brutal cold like pain through my body. It mixes with my other memories of hurt, and I wonder if I can ever really forget all the kinds of pain I've felt, if the memory will linger in my mind and on my nerve endings forever. In my head, I hear the *shick* of a blade, and I hear bells ringing, and I feel like I can hear Shirr screaming.

I'm running now, the air stinging my lungs as I suck in great, cold draughts and blow out clouds of steam. I try to calm myself, thinking: The walls I brush past, yes, those are real. My footfalls on the frosted road; real. The things I imagine are not.

I only know one place here on Vica. One person. She was a passenger on a ship I hitched a ride on once, and I know she can help me. There are places like it at every dock—they might be markets or hothouses or just alleyways of ill repute, where one can get illicit things. They pay off the Force to turn away from the trade, and you get a feel for where they are. They are easy to spot: There's always lurkers trying to sell you something, hawkers whispering about their wares, people shifting their eyes from side to side as they enter.

I'm not far from this one when I hear an "Oi!" and I slow immediately, but it's too late. I'd drawn attention to myself by running in the pre-dawn dark, and I see two Force officers, both looking pissed off to be on duty at this hour.

"You," one of them says. "ID scan. Now."

The old instincts kick in, and I leap into a sprint, the kind of fast-zipping, dodging sprint that comes from years of running away from the Force. Before, it was just life: run, get away. Now, I'm running toward something; I've got a purpose and a life to save, a life that would be ended if they found me wanting an Ident and slammed me in some frigid prison on this frozen port: one meal a day, a long sentence for lack of personhood, and all the time in the world to think about what Shirr went through before she was blown out of the airlock.

I don't lead the Force to my destination; that's a beginner move. You never run toward your target, always lead them away, lose them, and circle back. I take them past the market, close by Immigration but not too close, and then down to the landing pads with their great, grey cranes towering overhead. Five years ago, a Force grabbed me by my hood, and I twisted free of it, leaving them holding nothing but an empty jacket. I'd vowed to never let anyone get that close again, and I vow it again as I race through the dock, my lungs burning. There's no crowd to lose them in now, so I thread through tethers and around landing bays stacked high with cargo holds ready to be hitched to haulers. I can hear the *thud thud thud* of their boots behind me getting softer, further away.

Maybe I lose them, maybe I tire them out, maybe they just get sick of chasing some undocumented scrap of trash through the docks at this hour of the morning, but soon, I'm running from nothing. I collapse against a cargo hold, almost sobbing with relief, knowing that I just saved myself and Shirr from a fate that would end us both.

She is in the spot I remember, seated languidly at the front of a hothouse, the only building that looks awake at this time. It's an old building, brick, two stories tall and wide, with a balcony that wraps around the front and sides. The windows are all blacked out, the bricks painted black, but the porch is lit by large heat lamps to warm the flesh on display to passersby. There's no real middle to the arrangement on display, but she still seems to sit at the center, her rank obvious. Her long limbs are slick in a tight bodysuit and thick, black braids puddle around her seated form. She's dressed like any other hothouse flower, seated on the balcony and lit orange by the heat lamps, but she owns this place. When we met, she was traveling back from her grandmother's funeral. She'd sneak me cups of coffee from the galley and tell me stories of growing up on her nanny's farm on tropical Aleid before the ship's second-in-command would catch us and send me back to the cargo hold where I belonged.

"Uh, Phane?" I say, trying to catch my breath.

"Yes?" she says, her voice as smooth and the syllable as elongated as her form.

"Do you remember me? My name is Evey. We met coming back from—"

Phane laughs. "Ha! Of course I do. You are the little ship's mouse, scurrying back to the cargo hold, no? I offered you a job, but you said you liked the sky too much."

"Yes!"

"How can I help you tonight? Would you like work? My offer still stands."

I look to the others seated on the balcony, lovely-looking people in lace and leather and velvet, all gleaming in the heat lamps' soft orange glow, imagining myself as one of them for just a moment. I can't picture myself in their finery, and I shake the thought out of my head. I am not sure what I can say in front of them, so I ask the first thing that comes into my mind.

"Can I book you? Do you see women?"

"My sexuality is *money, miel,*" she says, the vowels rounded with her accent. "Do you have it? Money?"

I nod and she stands, towering over me on the raised balcony. She gestures for me to follow. I clatter up the steps behind her and hold out the account chip I took from one of Shirr's drawers. Phane's got her scanner poised for me, and it *tings* gently as the charge goes through. I have no idea how much Shirr has in this account, but it's enough for the cost of a ten-minute consultation, which is what I need to start.

Phane leads me through the hothouse, the shape of her disappearing now and then into the shadows of the tight hallway. The velvet of her catsuit bleeds into the darkness. She stops before a door and leads me into a large room, heavily accented with gold and red, the bed a centerpiece and laden heavy with furs and pillows.

"I don't want a service. I need a chip," I say as she shuts the door, no time for pleasantries. Phane looks me up and down, brings out a small detector from the cavern between her breasts, and checks me for surveillance, malware, and my Ident. Nothing registers.

"You're still undocumented?"

"Yes. I need the chip quickly. Pirate or built, whatever I can afford. It doesn't matter."

Phane isn't just the proprietor of the hothouse, or a flower; she's got her fingers in all manner of illicit trades. She offered to build me a chip when we met, but I didn't have the funds and wasn't sure I wanted one. Being legitimate felt too big, too much. Now, it's essential.

"Do you have the credits?"

"I have no idea. Can you check?" I wave the account chip at the detector, and she assesses the balance.

"This isn't yours," she says, not a question.

"No, but the person it belongs to wouldn't mind me using it. She needs help."

"I don't care anyway." She grins and looks at the detector. "You could get a built chip and an entire night with me with what's in this account."

"I don't have a night. I just need the chip," I say. A small part of me, the part not overtaken with panic and horror, wishes I did have the night.

"It will take a little while to build you a history." Phane goes to a gilded cupboard in the corner, where she pulls out a hand unit and a small, carved wooden box. "Take a seat, *miel*."

She gestures to the bed, and I sit, but can't settle. I worry the tassels of fabric between my hands. Phane presses an intercom and speaks softly into it, and in a few seconds, a young person comes through the door. They are slight, short-haired, with a strong nose and clad in a brilliantly gleaming gold dress. They introduce themselves as "Rene, they."

"My friend needs a chip," Phane says and places the tiny new chip into their hand. Rene sits at the small table in the corner of the room, sets the chip onto a reader, and it glows as they activate it.

"Name? Where were you born? What age are you?" Phane asks, as Rene enters commands with the practiced fly of hands that have made these motions many times before.

"Evey Et. Twenty-five. Wherever you like, I don't care about the specifics."

"You're from the Cult of Et?" she says, lifting one carefully painted eyebrow.

"Yes," I say, "that's why I'm undocumented. My mother was an acolyte."

"I've not met anyone who left that cult. Come by some other time, I'd like to pick your brain."

"Yes, of course." *Yes, yes, I'll do whatever you want; just code the chip!*

"Why now? What's the hurry?"

I put my face in my hands. "My friend, she's been taken. I have to follow her, find her. Can you get me listed on the crew manifest of a hauler at the dock? *The Algea?* Can you give me the credentials to fly?"

"You can afford that, so yes." She winks one of her liquid brown eyes at me, though they look black in the red light of the room. "*Can* you fly, little *souris?*"

"I think so," I tell her, trying to sound more confident than I am.

"It's not so hard. The ship does most of it, no? Now, who took your friend? The Force? Debtors?"

"A man. Just a man," I say, desperate.

"Men do these things, don't they?"

"There, Evey Et," says Rene. "You're now Evey El, nineteen, from Coliv. Parents deceased, no siblings. I've given you an extensive travel history, so it doesn't look suspicious. Where was the last port you called at?"

"Plano," I tell them. "We picked up tea and . . ." I don't know why I say it, but my mind's eye fills with the scent of the dried leaves and the image of steam coming off cups in the library, and I start to cry. Phane waves Rene from the room. She slips the chip into an implanter, and it hisses as it sterilizes the tiny bead. She holds up my arm, pulls my sleeve back, and fires the thing into my wrist. I feel it so deeply, but the pain is a balm. I ride it up and out, a brief moment of feeling embodied. Phane sits beside me, gathers me up in her arms, and lets me sob into her lap.

"It's okay, *miel,* this is on the house," she says, stroking my hair with the practiced touch of someone who has done this many times.

The Algea feels different without Shirr's presence. It's huge and empty, not homey like it was when she filled the space with her warmth, her endless kettle boiling and steaming cups of tea. I sit in the chair on the bridge and glance at the empty space on the control panel, aching to be there in the fold of warp, looking out at the curving stars while Shirr plots our course.

I wake the ship's system and scan my wrist, waiting for the clang and alarm of an error as it registers my new chip, but there is none. *Welcome, Evey* appears on the main screen as it accepts my credentials and opens to me. I scroll to the launch windows, snapping up the soonest—six hours time, which must be due to a cancellation as there are no more slots for another twenty-seven hours. I'm grateful. I can't imagine the things that Shirr might endure in twenty-seven hours, and how it would feel to wait.

Six hours still gives her enough time to suffer and me enough time to wait to feel my thoughts grow large and all consuming. I ache to feel the clang of the ferry as it locks onto the ship to take us to the launch zone, but each second drips by like thick oil. I try to hold them back, but memories flick through my mind: pain, darkness, the deepest loneliness I'd ever felt. Sounds like screams, like bells, like knives unsheathing. *Schick.* I wish I could knock myself out. I wish I could taste some of the sweet ni'ima I'd shared with a kid once in an alleyway in the docklands on some planet or another. We dripped the fluid onto our eyeballs and then lolled, so languid and thoughtless that I'd never touched it again for fear of never stopping. I remembered her eyes, tinted violet and empty, and saw myself that way so easily. Now, I'd do nearly anything for half a drop to ease this waiting agony.

Wandering through the halls of the ship, I pick up a book like I'm going to read it, like I would be able to keep my eyes on the words and absorb them. It's the one Shirr was reading, *A Tomb* by Essien Obe, and I think of her and the little huffing noises she makes when she's reading something she doesn't quite like and the way she lifts the page to move to the next one as she starts it, like she can't wait to move through the story. Like she's waiting for it to catch up with her. Then I'm crying into the pages, and I sink to the library floor, curling around the book, and I sob until the clank of the ferry bots locking onto *The Algea* shakes me out of it, hours later. It's time to launch.

———

The person across the comms asks me something. All I hear is the lift at the end of the sentence, so I know they are asking a question.

"Sorry?" I ask. I wasn't paying attention, too wrapped up in making sure I've got the launch plotted perfectly in my head.

"You're not carrying cargo," they say, no longer asking.

"No," I say, preparing my lie. "Family emergency. My sister's—"

"Launch sequence accepted," they interrupt, sounding bored and annoyed, and I'm eternally grateful that Launch Control doesn't care about the change to my logged itinerary, that my new chip doesn't send up any warnings, and most of all, that my launch sequence is sound.

My heart is beating up into my throat as the ferry moves *The Algea* into position, and there's a clunk as the launch fuel tank locks into place.

"Begin launch sequence," the voice over the comms says, and I want to vomit. I know that my launch protocol is sound, I've watched Shirr go through the steps so many times, but I can't help but think that I've forgotten something or that I've made some navigation mistake that will cause a catastrophic failure, make the ship break apart across the sky. From the captain's chair, where I'm strapped in so tight that my legs are starting to go numb, I press the little "enter" button under my index finger, starting the sequence. Beneath me, I feel the ship ticking, whirring, the engine building.

"Three, two, one, launch," the comms say, then *The Algea* roars to life, and I can't hear anything else but the scream of the engine, the air rushing against the hull. My stomach drops, and I'm sucked back into my chair as we rise, faster and faster. Everything rattles so hard that I can't believe the ship doesn't come apart, even though it's like this every time. My teeth knock together, and my chest feels like there's a crushing weight pressing down on it. I've got my thumb poised over the "abort" switch, ready for the ship to break up at any moment, but then the screaming air eases as we slip into the exosphere. The shaking stops, and all noise ceases as we leave the atmosphere, and there's a rush of relief that sings through my body as the soft silence of space enfolds *The Algea*. I launched the ship and survived! And then I think about how much more I'll need to survive from here, and it doesn't feel as good anymore.

I can't focus enough to read anything. I throw my book across the library, where it thumps against the wall and falls to the ground, split open. I go over to it and glance down at the pages, looking for portents in the printed words. There are none, though; it's just a random page.

Every grumble from the engine or creak of the steel sounds like a *shick,* and I can't do much besides stare out of the viewport, watching the stars bend around the warp bubble. I'm in an infinite limbo, the *whenwhenwhen* echoing in my brain, along every corridor of the empty ship.

It is no great surprise when the blip sounds, but I still almost jump out of my skin. I know it's him. I don't walk or hurry, I run. I sprint toward the controls, all the screens flashing with the distress warning.

I've been waiting to hear his beacon, but the reality of this confrontation creeps up my spine like a fire in zero grav. I've been waiting, and I won't ever be ready, but I don't have a choice. I lock in the coordinates, and the ship pilots itself through the black. I can't see anything yet, not even the far-away gleam of a hull or the blip-shine of distress beams. There's a deep silence in the ship, broken only by the tick in the engine. It's always so deadly quiet mid flight, but this feels different. Full, full of potential, none of it good.

There, on the front screen. A tiny glimpse of his ship, growing bigger. *He* grows bigger in my mind and my heart; an icy vise clamps quick and tight around my chest. *I don't want this, I don't want this,* but the ship grows in the view, inevitable. There's a dread certainty dripping through my veins, like I always knew this was coming, that when I blasted out into the void in the lifepod, it was only a matter of time before I'd be back on his ship again. I didn't imagine it being like this, but I knew deep down that I'd end up there.

The steel hull comes clear into view, a chrome crescent gently cupping the massive cargo load. It floats, mid-black, unmoving. A trail of air spills out from the hull. He's voided the atmo.

Shirr's backup evo suit is too tall for me and bunches at the ankles and wrists. It's old and barely used, smells musty, and crackles as I pull it up. I softly hope the seals haven't aged past use, then I click the helmet into place with soft, clumsy gloves, and it takes forever because my hands shake too much to make the seal.

I'm not here, really. I'm back in time, knife to my throat, and then I'm back further, warm, clammy hands on my cool skin; I'm back in the dark, with a hot-breath whisper in my ear, *Don't move, don't make a sound.* I move forward anyway, mouth gaping, with the confines of the suit closing in on me and the pump of the O2 feeling inadequate for the way I'm gasping. Then the ship jolts as it couples with his, and I almost rip out of my skin as it locks together. I get in the airlock, holding my breath inside the suit. The pressure in the lock stabilizes to whatever is waiting for me. I wait for the join to open.

I wait.

[5]

A wrench floats through the gap as the lock splits apart and clangs to the floor in my gravity, loud enough to quake me. He's disabled everything: the atmosphere, the OS, gravity panels, and the climate. His ship is dark, the only light coming through from our side, and in the borrowed glow floats everything that hadn't been fixed down. Tools, food, clothing. A filament rope coils slowly like a sea snake I saw in an old nature show. I fumble my thick-suited fingers and grab a torch out of the air as it passes by the lock. Didn't think to bring one.

I do not move, not wanting to start the chain of events that must inevitably follow. I watch the weightless tumble of detritus for too long until something sparks inside, and I take a step, and then another, like my feet belong to someone bigger and braver than me. I step from the pull-down of my gravity up into freefall, the weight of my body releasing in an instant. I swim forward, brushing a coverall, an MRE, and a rusted plier out of my path. There's the place where I smacked my elbow as I ran from him. I grab the doorway to his quarters, and I pull myself along, peering in as I pass. The bedsheets twist gently in the air, the pillow bumping off the ceiling.

The ship is still, devoid of movement, sound, of breath, except my own panting inside the helmet. Passing the sleeping quarters, I come to the storeroom door, the room he kept me in. I push the door open, shine the light into the gloom, and I push my horror, my *horror,* down and fold it into a box. There is no one there, nothing inside.

I round the hall to the common area, and a flock of cutlery gleams above the kitchen. It's empty. I pull a knife from the floating array and tuck it into my pocket.

Pushing myself off the wall of the common area and back into the hallway, I misjudge and slam into the hull, my body thumping hard against the steel.

"Fuck," I say, too loud, the sudden noise booming in my own head. The bridge door is halfway open, and I shine the light inside, the gleam spilling over the chair, the controls, the front view inky-black and scattered with stars. It's empty.

I look across the bridge to the lifepod. He's replaced the one I took; he had to—you can't get permission to launch without one. The replacement is from a different model, but the same make. It shines acidic yellow in the bay, looking incongruent against the dull steel of the bridge. The door to the pod is closed. I career toward it, pop the lock, and heave the door open.

There's nothing. They are nowhere in the hauler. That only leaves the hold.

I drag myself through the bridge and take off into his ship, heading to the hold. With my fat, suited fingers, I set the opener to manual, and it grinds up. I step inside the airlock and press the button to match the pressure inside the hold, and the outer door rises right away. Inside is a world I wasn't expecting. The cargo hold wouldn't usually have grav or atmo, so the freight is always locked in tight, but everything in here has been untethered. Giant cubes of minerals career silently off each other in the torchlight, behemoths bumping around the massive hold. I shine my light down the hold and see something white. Is it a suit floating and unmoving at the bottom of the hold? Is it him? Is it Shirr? Did one of the containers hit them? Are they dead?

I can't go in there. I'll die.

I have to.

I clip the flashlight to my shoulder and float into the hold through a wide space between the mineral containers, crashing into each other in perfect silence. I reach the outer wall, grab the handrails, and turn, beaming my light around, and I spot a cube bouncing off another and coming right toward me.

"Fuck!" I bellow and push off the wall, floating out of the way as the corner clips the wall right where I was. It ricochets slowly off into the hold. I scramble my clunky hands across the wall, pulling myself lower into the hold. As I take off, a container passes just above, and I reach out, pushing myself off it as it glides just overhead. It knocks into another, and the force of the collision tears a corner off. A rain of minerals pours out, curving out through the hole and twisting in the vacuum like a murmuration. I'm enveloped in stones, the smallest pinging off my helmet, the bigger ones thumping off my suit like body shots. I try to block the flurry by putting my hands up. It means I don't see the container until too late. It clips me, sends me spinning.

I'm careening blind, stones pelting into my helmet with a high rattle, the lower thump of them hitting my suit. Flashlight trails illuminate the hold in a jagged gleam as I spin. I bounce off another container and am sent whirling again. I'm headed toward two cubes moving close to each other, but I've got nothing to catch myself on. I throw up my hands, futile, and scream as I move between them. My hands brush up against both; they're so close. I pop out the bottom as they collide, and I'm about to release my breath when I hit another, bouncing hard off it so it feels like every bone in my body jars. I'm close to the suit floating at the bottom now. In moments I sail by it, fumbling with my thick fingers to catch it by the O2 tank, yanking it back along with me. Struggling to hold on, I bounce off another container, taking the impact in the shoulder, and I scream again with the pain that peals through me like bells.

The space is thick with minerals colliding. I pull the suit along behind me, then find the tether clipped to my side, tying it short with my clumsy fingers. Clipping it to the suit, I've got no time to check who is in it before a huge mineral chunk thwacks me on the side of my helmet, pulling me off the wall and jerking the suit along with me by the tether. We spin around each other, then they're dealt a full-body blow by the leading edge of a container moving downward, and I arc up and over, out of control. I hit the wall again, this time grabbing the handholds as I bounce off it. I pull the suit in close to me, then, hand over hand, we move toward the top of the hold, taking moments to avoid the huge stones, ignoring the constant soft crack of the tiny ones hitting us.

When we reach the airlock, I yank the suit in behind me, hitting the button to close the hatch. The small space glows in the torchlight, and I watch as a container approaches. The airlock closes just as it hits, denting the door inward. There's nothing but the sound of my breath inside my helmet. I grab the suit and pull it towards me, but when I flick up the visor to see into the helmet, my gut drops.

Inside the suit is a person I don't know, bruised and mutilated but still breathing. They're like a glimpse into an alt-universe where I didn't get away.

no, Evey, they're real. they have a name and a life, and they aren't just some symbol.

They rotate in the air, body still, and for a second, I think, *Fuck, I am too late,* but then they come to in a wild thrash, kicking out, flailing. When they've spent whatever is left, they curl into a fetal position, white-suited body turning slow revolutions in the middle of the airlock until the tether catches them.

I tie them in close and use the handholds dotted along all the walls to pull us through the hallway, propelling toward *The Algea.* When we reach our airlock, I take them into my arms, and once the lock pressurizes, I slam the door opener. As I step into the gravity, they sag against me as the grav panels drag us down. I hurriedly unsuit myself, throwing the components down piece by piece, and then I slip them out of the suit they're in.

Fuck, they're battered. I race for the medkit and cover them with a heat blanket, the plasticky fabric crinkling as I throw it over them. The IV kit finds their vein and feeds them fluid one drop at a time. I race to the library, looking for a book on trauma medicine that I know is there. I find it on a high shelf and jump to pull it down, page through it blindly, not even sure what I'm looking for.

When I look up, Shirr is there. Standing at the door to the library. So simple. She's not there, then she's there. My heart surges, and I throw the book down. I try to get up and run to her, but it's like something is holding me down, and she says quietly, "Evey . . ." That's when I hear the *shick* and realize that I can't get up because *he's* holding me by the shoulder. The cold sharp of the blade digs into my neck.

I don't move, don't make a sound.

It's a shock to feel him here again, in the womb of our ship, the place I've always felt the safest.

Shirr's glued to the spot like she's stuck on a glitchy grav panel. Her face is bruised, cut, and her wrists rubbed raw from restraints. He's hurt her, and it makes me want to kill him. He must feel some kind of surge in my body, because he pulls the blade across my cheek, blood spilling out in a hot little gush. I can't help but cry out. Shirr closes her eyes and moans, the noise escaping like she can't help it either.

"Open your eyes or I'll kill her." His voice pries up underneath me, wrenching me open to terror because I know what's waiting for me if I don't. The knife point digs into my neck again, the warm trickle of blood moves down my neck. Fuck. Fuck.

"You *want* me to watch, do you?" Shirr says, turning her face back to him, and she summons strength from somewhere deep. I watch it fill her. She's terrified, but still so strong. Where does it come from? Has she always had this bravery inside her? Do we all?

"What's the fun of having the power if nobody knows about it?" she says. "That's why you started dumping the bodies instead of just airlocking them. So everyone could see. Well, you got your wish because I *see* you. At the end of the day, you're just another violent man. The galaxies are full of them."

"You can't see anything!" he says, and his voice cracks a little at the end, betraying him.

I almost laugh. It's almost funny. The feeling of scorn shreds its narrow way through my fear, but I catch myself in time and just jolt a little in his arms, blade gripping the skin and cleaving it in a narrow sting. Fuck, Evey, don't do his work for him.

"Evey thinks you're empty, but you're not," she says, head still turned slightly to one side. "I think you're full; I think you're spilling over. But you're afraid, too. You're afraid no one sees you, or if they do, they could see that you're just as pathetic as the rest of us."

All the muscles in his body tense, a full-body windup that I feel in the press of his skin to mine. We're so close that I feel every heartbeat, every breath. His smell envelopes me, his heat. His rage-sweat drips down my neck. He feels real. So long inside my head, a stand-in for all the bad men on all the worlds, now he's here again, and he's a real, breathing thing. He's not a monster, something cold and slimy. He's just a man, a hot, sweating, heart-beating, real man. And Shirr's right. He's not empty. He feels strong and wiry against my back, breathing hard. He's quivering, surging over with rage.

No. With fear.

He's *afraid* of us.

Afraid of women who aren't scared of him or who are scared of him but bolster that fear with anger. And history. Women he can't turn into statues with his terror. Who knew it could be so simple?

His monstrosity dims. It's not the kind of seen he wants. He wants us to see the power he projects, not to see inside of him.

That's the thing about showing yourself; you can't control what people see.

"You're afraid of us," I say, acting braver than I feel. He grips my hair tighter, and I feel a clump of strands tear out. "You don't know what to do with live women, do you?"

"I know what to do with live women. And I know what to do with girls like you," he says, lips moving against my ear. It makes me shudder. "You're nothing. No one cares if you're gone. No one notices. One less hitcher-bitch in the docks. The Force should pay me. It's a valuable service."

"You think you get to do what you want with me?"

"I know it. You're nothing. You're invisible."

He's right. I am invisible. I've spent so many years as someone who normal people just wish wasn't there. Eyes slide right over me, like if they pretend not to see, they won't have to think about me and my miserable kind junking up the place with all the other garbage. But it doesn't mean I'm not a person. It doesn't mean I deserve to be used and wasted for this man's convoluted desires, my body floating out in the cold of space or discarded on a refuse pile.

"She's not invisible. I see her," Shirr says. She cracks an eye.

"You? You're just as invisible as she is, you wrinkled old bitch. I prefer women in their prime."

"You're wrong. *I'm* in my prime," she says. "And Evey? She's just getting started. You have no idea how powerful she's going to be."

"She won't live to see it," he hisses.

But he isn't going to kill me. Not yet. If I'm dead, he won't get what he wants, which is to see me suffer and make Shirr see me suffer. So, it doesn't matter what I do or say. He wants me alive to punish me, to punish Shirr.

"Eat shit," I say. He didn't think to search me, didn't expect me to fight back. I slide the knife from my pocket in a quick motion, then bury the blade in him as deep as it can go.

His wailing sounds less like pain and more like frustration. He lets me go because I've stabbed him in the groin, and the hot gush of blood that spills over my hand tells me I might have nicked his femoral artery. He clutches at the wound, applying pressure, and I race to Shirr.

"You *cunt*," he spits at me as I wind around Shirr and almost hide behind her. I can be brave in the moment, but once it's done and I hear the hatred curdling his words, I feel small and scared again. What do they say? *You can't be brave without fear?* I'm so afraid. I feel the blood sticky on my face, hear the *shick* of his knife, the sound of bells ringing in my head, making me dizzy.

He moves forward, we step back, and he slips a little in his own blood. Even though I'm still surging with fear and adrenaline, I almost laugh again. I wish it wasn't funny. I wish I wasn't here, watching his masks melt away before my eyes and finding it both terrifying and deliriously hilarious. It makes him more dangerous. We have the power now, but his power has curdled. He hated us before; now there's new depths to it. I get a quick flash of where I'd rather be, which is right here in the library but in a different context, with the quiet pump of air from the vents punctuated by the turn of pages, and it sends a pang of something through me— not just longing but a kind of strength.

I've got something worth fighting for. I'm not just scrambling to stay alive anymore. There's a life I want and a way I need to feel and *fuck him* if he thinks I'm going to let it go.

Shirr gently touches the wound on my face, and the sting brings everything into diamond focus. He's bleeding slowly, the blood pooling and spreading, coming closer to the edge of the ancient rug, to the piles of books on the floor. She whimpers like it hurts her to see anything of his marring the sanctity of the library. Then she runs down the hall, rattles in her sleeping quarters, and comes back with a lock box, fumbling the keys. I don't know what she's doing, but I help her with them. Inside is her blaster. I look at it, then to her. She takes it out, aims it. She has him in point-blank range, and she straightens her arms like she's coiling back to fire.

"I hate that you're turning me into a killer," she says, voice cracking.

"After everything I've done?" he asks.

"Especially after everything you've done. I'm not a killer. I'm not like you." She shudders with the horror of it, her finger squeezing tighter on the trigger. She screams then, and *I can't I can't I can't* see her like this, so I ease the blaster out of her hands and point it at him.

"I'm not a killer either," I say, coming closer to him, so close I can smell his sweat and feel the blue-hot fury coming off him, feeling less and less frightened the angrier he gets. I press the blaster right against his temple, where it skids against the sweat just a fraction. "Now MOVE," I say.

I push him with the blaster, trigger finger braced, into the bridge. To the lifepod. I need him away. I need him off this ship, the stink and aura of him gone from the one place I've ever felt wanted. He skids and limps, but when he gets to the seal of the pod, he digs in.

"No," he says, softly. Oh, now *he's* scared.

"Get in," I say. He shakes his head. I press the blaster so hard into his head that it splits the skin there.

"Please," he says.

"Ever gave anyone mercy when they said please?"

"YOU FUCKING BITCH—"

I laugh and shove him with my free hand. He slips again in his blood, falling backward into the pod. As soon as he is in, I slam the eject button, and the lock clangs shut. There's a hiss and a crack as the lifepod peals away into the black.

"Why did you do that?"?" Shirr says. "He could bleed to death, but he could get picked up . . ."

"What do you think his chances are anyone will stop for his signal? Fifty-fifty?"

Shirr collapses back against the curve of the wall. "Less."

The soaring adrenaline in me slows to a trickle. I feel wrung out, hollowed. I collapse next to Shirr, needing to feel her near me. The soft warmth that emanates from her is nothing like the furious heat of him. It's a comfort. It's the feel of a human, a real human, not someone twisted into a cruel shape. I hold a hand out to Shirr, and she takes it. We stay there, our rapid breath easing, the shrill jangle of our nerves jumping less now. Shirr looks down, kicks at something at her feet.

"What's that?" I ask.

She picks it up. It's a little silver box with a tumble of wires spilling out the side, the threads frayed and torn.

"That," she says, "is the distress beacon. From the life pod."

"I've always felt so untethered," I tell Shirr as we sit in our places on the bridge, her in the chair, me perched on the edge of the control panel. The stars curve in the view, elongated as they pass along the edges. Until now, we've been silent, unsure of what to say or do, riding on the absence of fear as the ship slides through space and time, far away from *him*.

"With no family or friends, you know? Like I could just float right up and off whatever world I'm on and into the atmosphere, into space. Like my footprints don't leave a trace on the ground."

"I know the feeling," Shirr says. We slip back into silence. It's a long time before either of us speaks. I rub a fleck of dirt on the diamond surface of the view. It suddenly seems so important that I get it off.

"He killed *himself*, you know," she says. "*He* pulled the distress beacon out of the pod. If we'd have tried to escape in it, we'd be dead too. Floating through the black in that coffin forever."

"I know," I say, still scrubbing at the spot on the view. I remember the endless days inside the pod, watching the gauges click down, the deep, black hole terror of the vacuum outside, and of the thing I was becoming inside. I don't know what would have been worse: dying in there or living in there. I try to grasp at any kind of pity for *him*, that same fate. I can't. If it was anybody else, I'd question my brokenness, the way I've learned to cast my emotions out into the black. But for him? I can't summon a pang of guilt. I didn't kill him when I slammed that eject button. He doomed himself when he crept onto *The Algea* as I moved through his ship, when he ripped the beacon from inside our escape pod.

The mark on the view pane won't come off. I worry at it with my nail, tunnel-visioned, and it finally comes free, leaving the front view clear. Clean.

Shirr pulls my hand away. The soft, dry feel of her hand in mine grounds me. The hushy pump of air breathes from the vents.

Down the hall, in Shirr's quarters, the person he'd harmed mutters in their troubled sleep.

we'll help them, when they wake. we'll talk them through it.

I can feel the sharp dig of the steel control panel beneath my thighs, my feet planted strongly on the floor.

"I'm your tether now, you know," Shirr says. "Your tether to life."

She's right.

I'm here. She is with me. The past tugs, the torrent of memories old and new, boxed and sent out into space, all clamor to come back in, but maybe I can unbox them. With her help. And she, with mine.

She is my tether, my connection to the universe.

"And I'm yours," I tell her.

ACKNOWLEDGMENTS

I'd like to thank everyone who read all the iterations of this story over the years: Meg Elison, Melissa Ferguson, Alison Evans, Maddison Stoff, Emma Wortley, Curtis Chen, Jae Foxglove, Charlie Jane Anders. Thank you to Corey Jae White for the feedback, the support, and for being my tether when I'm flying out into the universe.

ABOUT THE AUTHOR

Marlee Jane Ward is a writer and visual artist living on Wurundjeri Land in Melbourne, Australia. She is the author of the award-winning *Orphancorp* series. Her work can be found at *Terraform, Interzone, Apex, Aurealis, Overland, Meanjin, Kill Your Darlings,* and more. Her memoir, *Money for Something,* was written as Mia Walsch and published in 2020. She is currently living her dream of being someone's goth aunt.

www.ingramcontent.com/pod-product-compliance
Lightning Source LLC
Chambersburg PA
CBHW021339060726
47591CB00006B/2100